WAYNE'S MANNER

Tyler Huffman

Wayne's Manner

Copyright © 2020 Tyler Huffman

All Rights Reserved

ISBN: 9798665777627

Front Cover Art: Jordy Farrell

Tyler Huffman

This book is dedicated to

My Grandma & Grandpa.

Thank you for all the adventures.

Wayne's Manner

Chapter 1

The parking lot was packed as Roger Coen stood outside the Department of Motor Vehicles. He looked down to check his watch, it was a quarter past two. With it being after lunch and before people would get off work, Roger was shocked to see how long the line was. He looked around the parking lot and watched cars come and go. Roger wasn't sure who he was looking for until a rusted-out Ford Taurus came coughing up.

Wayne Morris leaned across the seats and looked up at Roger. He had a face full of scruff and wore a beanie slouching down off his head. Roger, wearing a suit, although too big for him and desperately needing help from any tailor at all, felt like he made a bad decision.

"Sorry I'm late, go ahead and get in line." Wayne hollered across his messy car. "I just need to find a place to park this beast." Wayne's car revved hard then finally clicked into gear and he drove off.

Wayne pushed past five or so people telling them he was Roger's lawyer. He reached Roger and went to shake his hand. Roger, hesitated, but eventually took Wayne's greeting.

"I'll totally give you a discount for your time. Got caught up with another client watching paint dry." Wayne explained with complete seriousness.

"How did you get into this line of work?" Roger nervously asked.

"Oh, you know, the typical story." Wayne spoke quickly as though to get through a speech he had performed countless times. "Never had a job, parents took care of me, they died, got their money, sold their house, lived off that, ran out of money, didn't want to work, and one day a buddy paid me to keep him company on a drive across the incredibly flat plains of Kansas and in that moment I knew I was onto something."

Roger nodded. "Well thank you. It is nice to have someone to talk to. Makes the time pass quicker."

Wayne scanned the crowd of others waiting to get zero customer service. They all stood along a line painted on the ground. This was clearly the cheapest solution to creating a line, which likely took the least amount of effort from the prestigious government employees who work there. Wayne could appreciate that. He had been there many times and was able to estimate the time of arrival to the front based on time of day, number of people, and even account for the one or two people who would always act like they had never experienced the DMV before.

"Do you get a lot of business?" Roger continued the same conversation Wayne had been through with nearly every first-time client.

"You'd be surprised how many people just don't want to be alone." Wayne smiled. "I'd say we have about an hour left, maybe longer if this man with the tapping foot tries to get a discount by complaining about the line. I'm sure he will. What do you do?"

Wayne unlocked the door to his apartment and using his shoulder he powered it open. This was typical of the time of year. He could call his landlord like his neighbors have, but that would require work and he was done with that for the day. He tossed his keys on the counter. You couldn't see the surface through all the piled-up junk mail with only the pizza coupons clipped out, but you knew it was there somewhere. Floating weekly ads just do not exist in the real world. The rest of the place was not necessarily dirty, but one could tell Wayne didn't labor over keeping it tidy. One place that resembled a human nest of sorts and that was his comfy chair. A hub for half-drunk sodas and various remotes, it was a home inside a home. Plopped down in the chair, Wayne pulled out his cellphone and listened to his voicemails.

"Hey Wayne, it's Mark. I moved again. Gotta wait around for the cable guy to show up. Could use you from noon to four this Thursday. I'll have pizza and beer per the usual. Thanks."

Wayne wrote it down on his calendar with a reminder to call Mark back later. The next message came from a woman with an incredibly raspy voice.

"Hey there. I'm lonely and could use a man like you to come over and play with my..." Wayne calmly deleted the message and clicked a button so the next message so would play on speaker. He made his way to the kitchen and pulled cold pizza and a beer from the fridge.

The voicemail started with a short period of silence after which an old man with a monotone, Lurch-like accent spoke.

"Mr. Morris, my client is in need of your particularly unusual service. Her name is Martha Fairweather and she is dying. She has requested your attendance at her bedside to accompany her in her final hours."

Wayne, balancing his pizza and beer in one hand, walked over to his phone, and leaned down to delete the message. Upon pressing delete there was a knock at the door. Wayne jumped and dropped his dinner in the seat of his comfy chair. The dilemma to clean up or answer the door first ran through his head until another knock came.

Wayne tried to see who it was through the peephole but couldn't see anyone. He opened the door and a man in a nice, but dusty looking 1950's era suit stood up from a kneeling position. The Suit Man handed him a flier for Chinese food delivery.

"You don't look like the usual guy who drops these off." Wayne said sarcastically while taking the flier.

"I assure you I do not work for General Wong's Chinese Buffet and Delivery." The Suit Man retorted with the same monotone accent as the one on Wayne's voicemail.

"Did you just call me?"

"Hours ago. The matter at hand is rather urgent. May I come in?"

"I don't want to waste your time. What you're asking isn't really my thing."

"Then let me be brief. In exchange for your time we are willing to pay double your normal fee." The Suit Man pulled out a checkbook.

Wayne paused a moment and looked at the checkbook. He hadn't seen someone carry a checkbook around with them in years. "I spend time with people who don't want to be alone during boring events like going to the grocery store. I don't watch people die."

"Three times the rate." The Suit Man flicked open the checkbook.

"Man, you could offer me five times the rate and I still don't think I'd be down for something so morbid."

"Alright then," the Suit Man began to write a number on the check. He ripped the check from the book and handed it to Wayne. "This should be well more than you will likely make in ten years doing the type of work you do."

Wayne looked at the check and read the number one followed by five zeros. His eyes widened and he stumbled back.

"All you have to do is sit with her until just before she passes. At that time, the nurse will come in and relieve you." The Suit Man handed Wayne a small card with instructions on it and walked away.

"Wait, I didn't say I would!" Wayne spoke up out of his trance.

"Everything you need to know is on the card." The Suit Man continued down the stairs and to his car, a genuinely nice 1959 Black Cadillac with white wall tires.

Wayne watched the Suit Man drive off and then he shut his front door. He made his way back to his comfy chair without taking his eyes off the unbelievable check. Stopping at the chair he reached down and picked up the pizza, which unfortunately had landed face down and took a bite anyway. He finished off what beer had not soaked down into the cushion and looked at the card. It read: Saint Mary's Hospital, Room 1031. Wait for the call.

Chapter 2

Wayne walked up to the nurse's station. He had not been in a hospital since his parents died and wasn't really sure of the protocol. He knew what room he was supposed to go to and passed a glowing map display on the way in. There was a nice big arrow showing him where he was in relation to the map, but he was not sure if he could just go to the room without getting tackled by three giant men wearing all white. The nurse at the desk was too preoccupied with her work to notice Wayne's approach. With the absence of a bell to signal his presence, Wayne stood quietly and waited for her to look up. Soon, a doctor walked up and sat a chart down on the counter.

"Could you make sure that Mr. Stephens gets twenty-five milligrams of Ibuprofen every hour? He has a history and I don't want to cause a relapse."

"Of course, Dr. Woods." The Nurse responded to the Doctor without ever looking up. Dr. Woods then left the chart and walked away. Wayne took a hint that she was never going to look up and spoke up.

"Excuse me. I'm here to see Mrs. Fairweather. She's in room 1031."

The Nurse continued to not look up. "And what is it that I can do for you?"

Wayne smiled, "Apparently nothing. Thank you." He then proceeded down the hall as described on the big glowing map.

He found it strange how many doors to patient rooms were just open allowing anyone who passed by to be able to look in and see someone in pain or even waiting to die. The elderly primarily made up this section of the hospital, many who did not have anyone by their side. For a moment Wayne felt bad accepting money from the Suit Man to come and sit with Mrs. Fairweather, however, after seeing "Albert J. Fairweather Memorial Wing" painted on the wall he changed his mind. This woman clearly was not hurting for the money she paid.

Wayne could not help but wonder why she would need to hire someone to come and sit with her. Surely with all her money there was someone in her life who loved her and would want to be by her side during this time. He could see Suit Man standing at the end of the hall outside of her room posted up like a sentry guarding Mrs. Fairweather with his life.

"Mister," Wayne realized he hadn't gotten Suit Man's name, "I'm sorry what was your…"

"She's expecting you." Suit Man opened the door to Room 1031.

Wayne looked inside and could tell Mrs. Fairweather had been there a while. The room was decorated in such a way one could hardly tell it was in a hospital outside of the constant beeping of machines and toxic orange hazardous material disposal bin hanging on the wall.

He noticed that she was asleep and looked back at Suit Man who simply shut the door behind him. Wayne walked slowly over to Mrs. Fairweather's side. There was a chair near the wall by the window and he sat down. It was clear across the room from Mrs. Fairweather's bed and Wayne felt like a stalker hiding in the shadows for his prey to get undressed. This thought he quickly tried to erase from his mind considering the present company's age.

Figuring it would probably be better for him to be closer to her for when she wakes up, Wayne stood up and grabbed the chair. It was incredibly heavy especially for a guy whose most intense workout was climbing up and down the one flight of stairs to his apartment twice a day. The only way he was getting that chair by her side was if he dragged it. He pulled on the chair and the legs let out an ear-piercing screech as they dug into the tile floor. Wayne stopped and quickly checked to see if he woke Mrs. Fairweather. She was still asleep which allowed Wayne to reformulate his plan. He would move the chair an inch at a time to minimize the noise dished out by the legs. Every little pull let out a baby screech and every single time he checked to see if he woke her. It took Wayne about thirteen pulls to get the chair to a close enough distance from the bed that he was not too far away or so close as to be right on top of her. He relaxed and started to sit down when Mrs. Fairweather jerked her head right at him.

"Boo!"

Wayne fell back into the chair sending it scooting back at least a foot. Mrs. Fairweather rolled around laughing and clapping her hands.

"I got you good, young man." Mrs. Fairweather managed to blurt out between fits of laughter.

"You weren't asleep?"

"Of course not. I've been waiting for our conversation for some time now. I wouldn't dare fall asleep and miss out on a single second of it."

Wayne looked over and saw a pudding cup. "So, what kind of pudding do they have you eating in this place?"

"People don't wait to have a conversation about pudding, my dear, but if you must know it's tapioca."

"What do you mean you've been waiting a while? Mister...your man only contacted me yesterday."

Mrs. Fairweather reached out for Wayne's hand. He offered it to her, and her frail hand grasped his with all the strength she could muster. "I've been planning on this day much longer than you realize. Now sit. We have so much to talk about and extraordinarily little time to do it."

Her voice was kind and had a familiar quality to it. Wayne was sure they had never met before, but it felt like they had known each other for some time.

"This was probably the most unusual request you've ever received, am I right?" She looked at him with such curious eyes as if he were a subject for her to study.

"Actually, one time I had a man hire me to sit next to him during a meeting at his company so that he had someone to show his inappropriate doodles of the company's CEO to without getting in trouble or risk anyone he worked with telling on him."

"How on Earth did he manage to get you into a meeting without someone asking questions?" Her question was so full of sincerity that Wayne was caught off guard for a moment. He was used to people asking him about his work, but they had always been as interested as if talking about the weather while on the elevator.

"He told them I was a foreign exchange intern, which was great because it got me out of talking to anyone else." Wayne explained. Mrs. Fairweather let out a sharp laugh, but it soon turned into a gravelly cough. "Mrs. Fairweather, are you okay?"

"Yes, my dear. Unfortunately, this is what dying is." She rubbed her chest and stared into Wayne's eyes. "Moments of joy interrupted by bouts of pain."

Wayne began to feel bad again about taking her money. All she wanted was someone to bring a little happiness to her before she passed. Why she chose him, Wayne wasn't quite sure. He certainly did not have any more interesting stories to tell. That was pretty much the extent of it outside of talking about his adventures in video games.

"You shouldn't feel bad about taking my money, dear." Mrs. Fairweather assured him. "It was important to me that you be here."

Wayne wasn't sure if he was doing something with his face to express how he felt or if she just had gotten lucky and guessed what he was thinking. "Why me?"

"I'm the one paying. I get to ask the questions." She quipped. "Why do you purposefully strive to live such a boring life?" She asked bluntly.

How does one begin to answer that question? It was not really something he had ever thought about. "I suppose doing nothing doesn't really bother me. I mean, I have to make money to live so why not do it with as little effort possible?"

"If you didn't need money would you live a more exciting life?"

"What do you mean? Like, go skydiving?"

"I mean would you actually live? Get out of your crappy apartment and seek experiences few others ever have." Mrs. Fairweather suddenly had a life about her that seemed as if the conversation was giving her some sort of youthful burst.

"I guess so." Wayne thought about the money she was paying. He could use that to never work again and play video games all the time.

"You can't just guess so when it comes to your life. Do you want to be where I am and look back at all those days you spent standing in line at the DMV sharing other people's boring moments? 'Oh, remember that one time the grumpy lady gave us two lollies each?'" She mocked.

"No, that sounds terrible."

"Then it's settled. After you leave here today you will strive to live a fuller life. Agreed?"

Wayne hesitated. What if he didn't do as she was requesting? How bad is it to lie to a dying woman? "Agreed."

"Now, don't just say it because that's what a dying woman wants to hear. I need you to mean it!"

Wayne reconfigured his posture and dug deep to bury that lazy thoughts of video game heaven and responded, "Agreed!"

"That's better. Now, if you would please excuse me and send my associate in?" Her demeanor shifted so quickly that it caught Wayne a bit off guard and took him a moment to understand what was going on.

"Sure." Wayne got up and she grabbed his hand. She looked at him with such love in her eyes that Wayne forgot for a moment they were strangers and that she was dying. He walked out into the hall and Suit Man walked immediately in without Wayne saying a word and shut the door behind him.

Several minutes passed and Wayne played a game on his phone which centered around a student driver trying to get his license by having to drive as recklessly as possible. Wayne had the top score in the world on the leaderboards. Suit Man came back out into the hall.

"She would like you to return now." Suit Man said and left.

Wayne walked back in and noticed that she was not looking near as good as she did when he stepped out. She barely lifted her hand off the bed for him to grab and he helped her the rest of the way using both hands to wrap hers around his.

"Remember our deal. Promise me that you won't break it." Her voice was weak.

"I promise."

She smiled and closed her eyes. The occasional beeping of the room abruptly changed to a long continuous beep and Mrs. Fairweather was gone. A tear formed in Wayne's eye. He held her hand long after it had gone cold.

Chapter 3

"You think the cable company makes you wait so long that you get incredibly bored, which forces you into a spiral of binge watching and web surfing to the point that you upgrade your package and pay them more money just to flick a switch?" Mark proposed his deep philosophical question while holding his beer an inch from his mouth. He waited to take a drink until Wayne snapped out of a long trance and responded.

"Or maybe they have no choice, but to offer you this particular service that not only enslaves you the customer to a boring couch potato lifestyle, but also one they are bound to by some greater cosmic power forever keeping us pacified and satisfied with leading adventureless lives. Forever doomed to die alone with nothing save the memories of fictional characters on TV." Wayne stuffed his face with a slice of pizza while Mark stared in shock, still not taking a drink.

"Man, you're a bit on the darker side today." Mark finally took a long swig of his beer. "Something going on?"

Wayne thought about telling Mark about Mrs. Fairweather and their brief time together in the hospital, but before he could the Cable Guy showed up.

"Hey man, you're cool to leave if you want. I'll chat up the cable guy for a bit." Mark placed his hand on Wayne's shoulder in an awkward attempt at comfort. "Maybe I'll pitch our theories to him about the enslavement of the human race and see how he reacts." Mark pulled out his wallet and began to count through his cash. Wayne got up and started to walk away. "Hey man! Don't forget your money!"

"This one is on the house." Wayne got in his car and drove.

Mark turned to the Cable Guy, "If you're in danger and need help just blink twice and I'll call the cops." The Cable Guy stared blankly at Mark. "Unless they're in on it. Blink once if they are." The Cable Guy tried hard not to blink and send the wrong message, but it was a hot and dry day and his eyes could not handle it. He blinked. "Dear, God." Mark's mouth dropped open and then he took a drink. "Want a beer?"

Nothing had ever really affected Wayne as much as what Mrs. Fairweather had said to him. He looked around his average apartment; the mail advertisement covered counters, the beer stained comfy chair, the entertainment center filled with the latest gaming and viewing technology. Typically, he would grab a beer and plop down in his chair and play video games for hours. Wayne had always believed that the journeys he took in the virtual world were enough of an adventure for him, but now they seemed a waste of time. Ignoring his game controller, he walked back to his bedroom and went to sleep instead.

His phone rang wildly. It was on full volume, something Wayne always set before going to sleep to ensure he would wake up for his appointments. He answered the phone and as he did there was a knock at the door.

"Hello?" Wayne spoke into the phone.

There was no response on the other end of the line. The knocking at the door continued. Wayne hung up the phone and stumbled to the door only to find Suit Man waiting on his welcome mat.

"What are you doing here?" Wayne was puzzled by Suit Man's visit. "Did you just call me?"

"You should be quicker to answer your phone. You never know the importance behind the call." The Suit Man remained serious as usual.

"What do you want?"

"May I come in?"

"My place is a mess, what's going on?"

"I'm here to inform you that you have been named in Mrs. Fairweather's will." Suit Man handed Wayne a document. "Please, come to this address tomorrow at 9 a.m. And be sure to pack a bag." He turned and walked away.

"What is that guy's deal?" Wayne shut the door and looked at the document. There was an address with a town name that he did not recognize. He pulled out his phone and typed the address into his GPS app. After a moment, the app indicated the address was to a general store an hour and a half from his current location. Wayne had no idea why Mrs. Fairweather would have left him, a stranger, anything in her will or even when she would have had time to do it. On top of all that to also ask him to drive an hour and half out of town to a general store. It was absurd.

He did a search for the town where the store resided and found remarkably little information except that it had a post office, an auto repair shop, and the general store itself along with a few other non-descript buildings.

As odd as the request was, Wayne checked his calendar and had no appointments the following day and decided that he would take the trip to 9711 S. Grey Crow Rd. Ramble Ridge, Oklahoma.

The drive made him wish there were someone like him he could have hired to keep him company. Oklahoma's highways, while not nearly as flat and straight as Kansas, were still full of their lackluster parts. Wayne especially found the seemingly never-ending construction to be the best part. These regular orange cone lined stretches of road added another thirty minutes to his drive.

Wires crisscrossed his dash and console. His 2002 Taurus came fully equipped with a radio and tape deck player. This made listening to his tunes from his phone as easy as purchasing a cassette with a headphone cord attached that slid comfortably in the tape slot. With only the minimal sound of tape turning underlying every track, Wayne had himself an endless supply of music and podcasts. That is, if he kept the phone plugged into power via the cigarette lighter port. With all the cords used to operate this situation, Wayne's car looked like what bird's nest will be made of in fifty years.

Occasionally, mid song, his phone operating system's personality would chime in with an update on the directions. It was always so many feet until he needed to make a move, however, the roads not being lined with yardsticks made knowing the distance harder for Wayne. Whenever Wayne would hear her voice, he would turn down the music, grip the wheel with both hands, and glue his eyes to every street sign he passed to make sure he didn't miss any important information. This was yet another reason that having some company would be nice. A pilot always needs their navigator.

The town of Ramble Ridge snuck up on him despite his attempt at eagle eye vision. Much like his internet search displayed, there was nothing more than a post office, an auto shop, and the general store. None of the buildings appeared to be open. He pulled up to the general store, "Miss Sally's One Stop." Wayne could not see anyone inside, and the door was locked.

Wayne walked across the street to the post office, which was also locked, as was the auto shop. How could all these places be closed 9 a.m. on a Friday? Tired of sitting in the car, Wayne mounted up on the hood and waited for who he assumed would be the Suit Man. An hour passed and he had not had anything to eat all day. He assumed that the general store, Miss Sally's One Stop, would be open and he would be able to grab something there. Wayne leaned on his windshield and held his grumbling stomach.

"My apologies."

Wayne shot up and fell off the hood and landed hard on the ground. Face to face with the toe of a wing tipped pair of shoes, Wayne pushed himself up and dusted off his jeans as the Suit Man waited just as stoic as ever.

"You scared the crap out of me."

"I apologize for that as well." The Suit Man offered Wayne a handkerchief. "We had a bit of trouble at the estate getting it ready for your arrival."

"Estate? My arrival? What are you talking about?" Wayne looked around for a house, but all he could see were trees and fields.

"This should clarify a few things." The Suit Man handed Wayne an envelope stuffed with papers.

"Listen, man. Why can't you just tell me things? You're always handing me paper with instructions on them." Wayne waved the folder around.

"Please, get in your vehicle and follow me." The Suit Man turned and got into his 59' Caddy. Wayne examined his rusted pile of junk and felt a strong feeling of shame and depression and then got in and followed the Cadillac out of the small parking lot.

Just past the auto shop was a turn into a densely wooded area. The road was narrow but offered an exceptionally smooth ride. Wayne fell into a trance while driving along the winding road behind the sharp tail fins of the Caddy.

The trees began to thin out and Wayne could see through them on both sides much easier. He could not make out much detail, but one site that was noticeably clear was a small graveyard that appeared to be untouched for at least one hundred years. There were other small buildings and wooden structures along the way. He counted at least three small rocking horse style oil derricks, a common sight in Oklahoma. Occasionally the road had brief moments where it became wider as if to allow oncoming traffic to pull over so other cars could pass. Finally, the tree line stopped, and a long vast courtyard appeared.

The stonework of the walls and ledges that lined the gardens were intricate and clearly created by a master craftsman. Every flower and plant beamed with vibrant color. There was so much to take in at once that Wayne almost didn't notice the red of the Cadillac's tail lights flash in front of him. He smashed down on his brake pedal just in time to come within inches of the classic car.

Wayne hopped out quickly and started to apologize to the Suit Man as he checked to see if he had caused any damage. The Suit Man did not appear rattled by the exchange one bit. Wayne looked past The Suit Man and marveled at the mansion that stood before him. He had seen big houses before that in his youth he would refer to as mansions, but nothing compared to this. The building was nearly the size of a football field and looked like it had been transported from the Royal countryside of England.

A small group of people exited the main door and stood in a line at the bottom of a small, but grand in scale, set of steps. Each person was dressed for what Wayne could only assume was their position at the estate. One looked like a butler, one a maid, and the last a gardener. The Suit Man joined them in line.

"Welcome to your home, Mr. Morris." The Suit Man gestured with his arm in presentation of the massive house that stood behind them.

Chapter 4

Wayne was speechless. He wasn't sure if he had heard the Suit Man correctly. What did he mean by calling it his home? There was no possible way that Mrs. Fairweather left him her home in her will. She barely knew him. Wayne thought about it for a moment and realized that it appeared that Mrs. Fairweather didn't really know a lot of people or else she wouldn't have hired him to sit with her at her death. Now Wayne could only think about what amazing good he must have done at some point in his life to win such a lottery as to be given a football stadium of a house, if it was actually his house that is.

"Home?" Wayne managed to mutter out.

The man dressed like the butler stepped forward. He was an older man, quite possibly older than Mrs. Fairweather herself. His hair was grey and covered his head sparingly, but it was combed neat and nice, nonetheless.

"The name is Morese, Sir. Would you mind opening your trunk so that I may retrieve your bags?"

Wayne fumbled with his keys, dropping them on the ground. He bent down to retrieve them and was met by Morese who had already picked them up and popped the trunk open. Morese stood next to Wayne with his arm outstretched and the keys hanging delicately between Morese's thumb and forefinger. Wayne reached for the keys and upon taking them Morese was off to the rear of his car.

"Thank you, Morese." Wayne watched Morese stare perplexed at the inside of the trunk, reach inside, then pull out an old dirty backpack.

"Is this all, Sir?" Morese held the bag out just as he had done with the keys except this time it seemed he was doing so out of disgust.

"Yes," Wayne turned to the rest, "I'm sorry, I didn't realize I was expected to be staying long."

The woman dressed like a maid walked up, popping her hips side to side. Her clothes and body had every look as if she walked right out of a pin-up magazine except that they belonged to a woman clearly in her late sixties. "Ginger, at your service, Darling." She passed her hand over his shoulder and down his chest very seductively. "Don't you worry bout a thing. We will have your things picked up and delivered first thing tomorrow." She moved her hand back up his chest and with one finger played with the stubble on his chin. "Why don't you follow me. I'll give you the dime tour." She flicked her finger off his chin like she was striking a match and walked up the steps to the main doors.

"If we're all done here, I have a good bit of work to be doing." The man dressed like a gardener spouted off. The Suit Man nodded to him and he stomped away.

"Don't you mind grumpy old O'Conner. He's had a bug up his butt for decades now." Ginger quipped as she opened the door. Morese walked up the steps past Wayne and stood with Wayne's backpack at the top waiting for him to go in first.

Wayne made his way up the steps and stopped at the Suit Man's position.

"You will need to sign the papers I gave you in order for this to all be official." The Suit Man expressed with importance. "I will be by tomorrow morning to pick them up. Until then, try to relax and make yourself at home." He then left Wayne's side and drove away.

Wayne turned back to Ginger and Morese and slowly walked into what apparently was his new house. What he saw was unlike anything he had ever seen before in a house. The items on shelves and hung on the walls seemed like they would be more suitable for a museum, but here they were covering nearly every square foot of Mrs. Fairweather's estate.

"Was Mrs. Fairweather married to Indiana Jones?" Wayne joked.

Morese looked at Wayne with a stone-cold glare. "No, Sir. She was married to Mr. Fairweather for fifty years. She never took another lover."

"It was a joke." Wayne tried to explain himself. "Okay. Clearly you don't do humor. Noted."

"I will place your...book bag in your room. It is up the stairs and to the left. Take another left, then your second right, and the door is at the end of the hall." Morese explained using his free hand to illustrate the directions. "If you take the first right you will find yourself hurdling to your death down the elevator shaft. It is in the need of service, but due to recent events has yet to be seen to. For that I do apologize." Morese walked off and before Wayne could say thank you, he was already gone.

"He's quick." Wayne said to Ginger who seemed to be adjusting her eyes in the reflection of an incredibly old crystal vase.

"What?" Ginger stopped and spun around. "Yes, he takes his position very seriously." One of Ginger's eyebrows seemed to be higher than it was earlier, but she didn't seem to be intentionally raising it.

"Are you alright?" Wayne asked with great concern.

Ginger covered her eyebrow quickly. "Yes, of course. If you need anything all you have to do is press the button with my name on it on any of the panels that you'll find in every room of the house." Ginger walked over to a panel that had five small brass buttons on it. The second one said Ginger. She demonstrated using her free hand. A sort of seafaring tone played throughout the house. "I hear that, and I will be to you as soon as possible."

"Do all the rooms play the same tone for you?"
"Yes."
"Then how will you know which one I am in?"
"Don't you worry about that. I'll know." Ginger smiled and winked using her available eye and pranced off.

Wayne stood alone in the great entry hall surrounded by items from civilizations he had only read about in school and some he couldn't place even if he tried to Google them. He wasn't sure what to do so he just stood there in silence.

The doorbell rang. It was a deep, organ like sound. Wayne was so taken off guard by it that he nearly fell over. He headed for the door, but Morese beat him to it. Wayne stopped as the door opened and standing on the porch was an oddly attractive young woman in the way that you know you are attracted but can't quite figure out why. Her hair was dark, and she wore her glasses on top of her head like some sort of head band. She had big bubbly eyes and a button nose and when she looked in at Wayne her lips stretched ear to ear and revealed her crooked smile. Wayne starred like an idiot until she broke eye contact and turned to Morese.

"Hi, Morese! It is so good to see you again." Her voice was soft, but loud.

"Hello Miss. Parker. It has been some time." Morese responded with a familiarity in his voice.

"I brought cookies!" The young woman raised a plate of cookies up by her face. The joy she had in that moment was one you wished you could capture in a photograph to revisit anytime you want. Sadly, just a picture alone would not do it justice.

"Excellent, I will take these to the kitchen and put them on a proper platter right away." Morese took the plate that was wrapped in cellophane. He avoided the wrap as if it would burn him to touch.

"But that's my favorite plate." Miss. Parker showed a deeply sad side of herself in the moment but snapped out of it and turned to Wayne. "I'm Josie. I'm your new neighbor. Or you are my new neighbor. Either way. Hello!" She reached out her hand.

Still trying to take in everything about her from her short summer dress to her old lace up sneakers, Wayne hesitated before finally accepting her greeting. "I'm Wayne. Does everyone know about Mrs. Fairweather's will around here?"

Josie stepped further into the house, dropping Wayne's hand as her attention shifted to the walls. "Wow, it is just as I remember."

"You've been here?"

"Ages ago." Josie looked as though she was about to tear up, but wiped her nose, turned, and stood at attention in the cutest way possible. "Well, I'm sure you have some moving in sort of stuff to do. I'll leave you to it." Josie dropped her head and scurried to the door.

"You don't have to…"

"It was really nice to meet you, Wayne." Josie smiled and performed a sort of half curtsy then hurried off with a bounce.

"…leave just yet." Wayne stumbled due to such a sensory overload the day had been so far and decided he better find his room and lie down for a bit. As he made his way up the main flight of stairs he began mimicking Morese's hand movements to try and remember the directions he gave and to not fall to his death down an empty elevator shaft. Left, left, second right, straight.

Chapter 5

Wayne's room was twice the size of his apartment. It was decorated primarily in old maps framed and hung on the walls. They seemed to represent ancient empires and modern countries with outdated borders and names. The strong museum vibe about the entire house did not end here. Wayne reached out with his fingertips hovering close to a statue of a tiger but pulled his hand away before they entered its great big mouth. You're not allowed to touch in the museum.

He decided it would be okay to lie down on the bed because what is the point of a bed if you are not allowed to sleep on it. He stared up at the ceiling that appeared to consist of an epic piece of art carved out of a single huge chunk of wood. It seemed to tell a story about a young knight who was depicted holding together what looked like two halves of the moon. There were other small reliefs showing dragons, witches, ghouls, and griffins as well as clocks, potions, swords, and shields. Wayne wondered how long it must have taken the artist to create such a massive piece of work.

Not sure what to do with himself he pulled out his phone only to find it had zero service and no connection to a wireless router. He got up and walked around the room holding his phone up and out looking for a cell signal ignoring all the trinkets on the tabletops and items on the walls. They were just background noise. It smelled fragrantly nice in the room, for an old house.

Wayne was not having much luck finding a signal and stopped and noticed something very much worth his attention. A sword hung on the wall near the armoire. The blade was very reflective, and the hilt was wrapped in a bumpy green leather. It hung on a wall mount shaped like a claw. The claw looked like it could have belonged to what must have been the largest eagle ever. However, this eagle's feathering around the ankle shimmered red, orange, and yellow. Clearly just for decoration.

Wayne really wanted to touch the sword. You see a sword like that held up by a claw, you must touch it. He paced back and forth along the floor in front of the sword without taking his eyes off the blade. From time to time he would stop, tap his foot, and then continue.

"Screw this. My house. My stuff." He finally said to himself and out loud, because, why not.

He reached to take the sword from the wall but could not reach. Looking around he found a chair sitting near the north window. It may have been the East window or South or West for all he knew, but saying it was the North window sounded more fitting of the new owner of such a grand house. At least for inner monologue purposes. The chair was heavy and looked like it was made of the same wood as the art on the ceiling. He knew dragging it was the only opinion. Dragging chairs had quickly become a specialty of his. Wayne noticed the red leather of the seat and decided he should probably remove his shoes first, so he sat down in the chair to do so. Upon the very moment his butt barely encountered the chair, the room filled with water and Wayne began to float off the seat. Once his butt was no longer touching the chair the water vanished and Wayne fell to the ground. He jumped up and turned to look around. He was fine and still in his room. Nothing appeared to be soaking wet, which calmed him down. However, he did notice smoke coming off a candle, but couldn't remember if the candle was previously lit. The strangeness of the house was getting to him.

Standing, he kicked off his shoes and stepped up on the chair's arms carefully hoping to not have another strange vision, as if it were the chair itself that even had caused the first one. Once he was standing on the chair nothing happened and he reached for the sword again. The moment his fingers touched the bumpy green wrap, the claw mount seized up around the hilt tightly. Wayne fell off the chair and onto his back. He looked up at the sword firmly grasped in the eagle-like claw.

"Okay, so apparently touching things definitely isn't allowed."

Wayne's stomach rumbled and he realized he had yet to get anything to eat and must be going into a hunger delirium. Either that or he was just going crazy.

He got up and walked toward his bedroom door and noticed the panel of call buttons on the wall. For a second, he thought about ringing Morese or Ginger to bring him something but turned and saw the claw still holding the sword tight and decided he would leave and fend for himself. Wayne walked out of the room and shut the door. Upon the latch clicking in the door jamb the claw released its grip and the sword went back to hanging freely as a single drop of water dripped off the blade.

Chapter 6

The kitchen was just off the main entry through the formal dining room and past two swinging doors. Everything was stainless steel and the floors were white subway style tile. He looked around at the various cooking equipment and only was able to recognize the stove. There did not appear to be a microwave in the room, which was a major bummer for Wayne since that was the only thing he knew how to use. With his stomach rolling he desperately searched for the fridge. What he found seemed like it belonged in the White House because it was four times the size of any fridge he had ever used or even seen before.

He pulled open the massive doors and was face to face with hundreds of different ingredients, none of which were ready to eat in the cold pizza sort of sense. Shutting the door, he felt his stomach and decided he would buzz for Morese when out of the corner of his eye he saw the cookies Josie brought over sitting neatly on a platter on the counter. He rushed over and shoveled three cookies into his mouth while grasping two more in each hand. After a couple minutes of gorging himself on homemade chocolate chip cookies he realized that the platter was not what Josie had brought them over on. Looking around the room he finally spotted her plate waiting beside the door with a note card on it that read, "To be returned" in very elegant handwriting.

Wayne walked over and picked up the plate. There were roses circling the perimeter of the dish with little cats of different types between each one. Wayne laughed and coughed up some cookie causing him to choke. He dropped the plate on the counter. It bounced and flipped over while Wayne rammed his chest against the countertop edge to force the piece of cookie out. The cookie came out quickly and with little effort. Wayne had learned to give himself the Heimlich maneuver because choking on his food was a weekly occurrence for him. Catching his breath, he noticed there was another note taped to the bottom of the plate. This note was in a different handwriting that was much messier than the other, but still nicer than Wayne's.

"Hey New Neighbor. If you're ever lonely in that big ol' house or want to go on an adventure, give me a call. Hugs and Kittens, Josie."

Wayne blushed and could feel a smile on his face that hurt his cheeks. He tried to shake it off, but apparently you can't shake off involuntary emotions. He looked at the number she left and pulled out his phone. Still, he was without service. With the plate in one hand and his phone in the other he reached up, shaking his phone trying desperately to get a signal. A voice came from behind him.

"You look like mi abuela when she's trying to scare the birds from her tomato plants."

Wayne jumped and dropped both the plate and his phone. "Why am I so jumpy lately?" Wayne then looked down and saw Josie's plate in pieces on the floor.

"Lo siento, Senór. I did not mean to scare you."

Wayne turned around to see what he considered to be one of the most attractive Hispanic men he had ever seen, and that included Enrique Iglesias.

"Me llamo Santiago Alano Cortez. I am the one and only Master Chef of the Fairweather Estate. At your service." Santiago flashed a smile that made Wayne feel a funny feeling inside. "You Senór are hungry. I can feel it."

"I'm...I'm fine." Wayne struggled to wrangle his words. "I just had like twenty cookies."

"Nonsense. Cookies are not food. They do not bring you life." Santiago pulled a large knife from a block and threw it in the air. "Only death." The knife spun in the air like a fan blade on high. Wayne felt every part of his body clinch up. Once it reached the apex of his flight, the knife began its descent right into the delicate hands of Santiago Alano Cortez. Handle to palm of course.

"Okay, sure." Wayne panicked. He was still hungry, but now felt obligated after witnessing such an incredible trick. "I'll take a grilled cheese sandwich." Wayne requested.

"A grilled cheese?" Santiago leaned over the counter. His eyes fixed on Wayne.

"Is that okay?" Wayne was getting scared that he may have offended him.

"Be still!" Santiago shouted with a very gentle yet assertive voice. "I am scanning your soul."

Wayne looked down at himself, "For what?"

"For the spirit of the child you have captured and are holding hostage within."

"I have not captured any children. I promise." Wayne began to sweat. He watched Santiago's other hand inch closer with knife sticking out toward him. "Why, would you think that I have?"

"Because, no grown man would ever ask another grown man to make him a grilled cheese sandwich." Santiago's hand gripped the knife, "Unless of course..." He placed the knife one a chopping block delicately.

Wayne swallowed hard, "Unless of course what?"

Santiago stood up and smiled again, "Unless of course you hand some premium honey baked ham with jalapenos fresh from the garden on artisanal wheat bread baked fresh this morning served with a side of tomato soup made from tomatoes sent to me by my dear abuelita Rosa." Santiago flipped the knife up with one hand and pulled out a loaf of wheat bread from under the counter with the other.

Wayne let out a huge breath and laughed. "Wow, yeah that sounds great." He leaned down to pick up the pieces of Josie's broken plate from the ground and his phone. "I thought you were going to…" Santiago chopped down into the bread. Wayne jumped up quickly. "…kill me."

"No, Senór. Why would I want to kill you? After all, you are my employer now. That is not a very smart business strategy, wouldn't you say? Santiago moved around the room from counter to fridge to stove quickly, but with a slight dip in his step.

"Are you okay?" Wayne pried.

"Of course." Santiago applied butter to the bread. "Why do you ask?"

"You seem to be limping."

"Ahh si." Santiago walked out from behind the counter and under his apron Wayne noticed the presence of a prosthetic leg. "I lost it in the jungles of Borneo while searching for a rare herb I needed for an incredibly special sauce I was crafting. I had just found it when a Sunda Clouded Leopard jumped from the brush and tore my leg clean off. I reached for my rifle and targeted the creature right between its eyes. My leg dangling from his jaw, my finger on the trigger. I was ready to shoot, but then it spoke to me. He was only trying to feed his family. They had been driven from their home due to deforestation and food had been scarce. My leg would sustain them for at least one more week. I lowered my rifle and allowed the leopard to leave in peace with my severed leg. It thanked me and offered me a great gift. One of which I cannot speak of. Luckily, Mr. Fairweather was also in the jungle that day and came upon my weak and near lifeless body. He bandaged me up and carried me back to camp. It was there I offered my service to him and his for as long as I may live." Santiago flipped the pan and Wayne's grilled cheese flew and landed on a plate in front of the mesmerized Wayne.

"Wow." Wayne just stared at Santiago's prosthetic leg. "That's amazing."

"Yes. A couple years later that section of jungle was nearly completely wiped out and Mr. and Mrs. Fairweather had that very leopard and its family transported here to the estate where they live to this day."

Wayne choked on his sandwich. "Excuse me?" Wayne muttered through a full mouth of cheese, bread, and ham.

"Enjoy your meal, senor. We will talk more another time. Is there anything else I can do for you?"

"Oh, um, yes! Do you have a landline phone around here? I can't get a signal."

"Of course. It is right behind you on the wall." Santiago pointed. "It is the bright green relic right there. Hard to miss."

"Well, now I feel like an idiot." Wayne turned and went to the phone. He picked up the receiver and listened for a dial tone. On the other end he could hear Morese and the Suit Man talking, but in a language, he did not understand or had ever even heard before. He hung up the phone. "It's busy."

Wiping down the counters, Santiago pulled a cell phone from his pocket and tossed it to Wayne. "Here, use mine."

"Thanks, but there's no service out here."

"Ahh. On the contrary, Senór. You must first appease the cell tower up on the roof."

Wayne laughed, but stopped after looking at Santiago's profoundly serious face. "Appease the cell tower?"

"Si."

"How do I do that?"

"That is something you must figure out for yourself." Santiago finished cleaning up. "Just leave the phone on the counter when you're done." He threw his towel over his shoulder and walked out.

Wayne looked at the full bars on Santiago's phone and then at his own with no bars. He picked up the piece of Josie's plate that was still together due to the note being taped to it. Using Santiago's phone, he dialed her number.

"Hello!" Josie's voice blasted through the phone's speaker.

"Josie? Hi, this is Wayne…"

"Yeah! Hi, Wayne. Did you enjoy the cookies?"

"A little too much. Listen…"

"I'll be right over!"

"Oh. Okay. Great."

Wayne pressed the end call button and precisely five seconds later the doorbell rang. He rushed out through the formal dining room and into the entry hall to find Morese opening the door and Josie running in.

"What's the adventure?"

Wayne, still in shock at the speed of both Morese answering the door and Josie coming over, stood silent.

"Will you be needing anything else, Sir?" Morese said while shutting the door.

Wayne snapped out of his shocked daze. "Oh, no. Thank you, Morese." Morese gave a slight bow to Josie and walked away.

"I didn't say anything about an adventure."

"There's always an adventure." Josie twirled around the room.

"Well the cook…"

"Oh, I love Santiago. He makes the best spaghetti and meatballs. I think he has a portal to Italy or something because you can taste the authenticity."

Wayne struggled to match Josie's energy. "Well, he said something about pleasing a cell tower so I could get reception on my phone."

"It's on the roof!" Josie jumped and shouted.

"Yeah, but how do you please a cell tower? It's a tower."

"I don't know, but let's find out." Josie ran up the stairs and made a hard right and ran right up to an armoire. She flung open the doors and looked inside.

"Do you need a jacket?" Wayne slowly followed.

"No," Josie spread the jackets aside in both directions, "this is where the ladder to the roof is."

Wayne walked up and looked in the armoire to find a long metal ladder leading straight up. "Wow. Secret ladder? This is just like a videogame."

"I've never played a video game." Josie said nonchalantly.

"You've never what? Never mind. How did you know this was here?"

"I used to play here as a kid." Josie's mood dropped like a stone in the sea.

"Oh man. I'm sorry. I didn't mean to bring up bad…"

"It's okay!" Josie perked up like nothing happened. "Let's go!" She grabbed onto the ladder and started up. Wayne paused a moment and watched her disappear into the dark.

"Josie?" He did not hear a response. "Josie?" Still nothing. "Man, I hope it's not very tall." Wayne entered the amoire and headed up after Josie with very timid steps.

Chapter 7

The ladder to the roof stretched higher than Wayne could see. He knew it was a three-story house and assumed there was some sort of attic space like most houses, but his climb seemed to be taking much longer than what he expected. It was completely dark, and Wayne made his ascent on feel alone. He couldn't see Josie but could hear her steps. She seemed to be moving at a much faster pace than he was. Wayne continued to climb, but soon realized he could not hear her anymore. He stopped so not to run into her and latched onto the ladder.

"Josie?" Wayne's voice echoed up the chamber. Nothing. "Don't mess with me Josie. I'm not the biggest fan of heights." Wayne hollered. "Or surprises!"

A loud boom shot through the shaft and Wayne closed his eyes as if he could even see anything with them open. After the echo of the boom subsided, he heard a long screech. He opened his eyes and saw a small crack of light up ahead.

"Man, this hatch is heavy!" Josie yelled. "Hurry up here and help me."

Wayne saw Josie's hair fall in front of the crack of light and in a way, it was sort of beautiful. He released his death grip on the ladder and continued up. His hand grabbed her foot as his head bumped into her butt. This let him know with intimate certainty that he made it to her.

"I'm so sorry"

"Here, climb up beside me and help me push." Josie scooted over to one side of the ladder.

Wayne, careful not to inappropriately touch her again shifted his way up on the other side. It was a tight fit. He could feel her breath on his face and her chest pressed against his. His hands started to sweat, and it made his grip far less strong.

"Are you ready?" Josie whispered knowing Wayne was only inches from her face.

"Yeah." Wayne said with his face down because he feared he had bad breath and did not want to blow it right into her nose. "Why are you whispering?"

"You're so close to me. What's the point in being any louder?" Josie said logically.

"Fair enough." Wayne whispered back.

They both pushed up on the hatch and it swung up and over, smashing into the rooftop with a bang. Everything was now illuminated, and Wayne and Josie's relative positions were much more awkward than they realized.

"Ladies first?" Wayne uttered nervously.

Josie smiled and pulled herself up and out of the shaft only to lean back in and offer a hand to Wayne.

He dusted himself off and noticed just how dirty Josie had gotten. There was a thick line of dust and dirt down her back.

"You're really dirty too." Wayne told Josie. She looked down and didn't see anything on the front and looked at Wayne quizzically. "Your back." Wayne clarified.

"Oh!" Josie laughed. "Do you mind?" She turned her back to him so that he could dust her off. Wayne awkwardly moved over to her and gently patted her down. Josie did not seem to mind being touched by what was pretty much a stranger as she just looked around the roof and finally up toward the sky. "There she is!" Josie pointed and moved away from Wayne as he still was cleaning her off.

Wayne looked up at what she was pointing at and saw the cell tower. It was huge and looked like a replica of the Eiffel

Tower, but all silver. He did not remember seeing it when he drove up, but then again there was a lot to take in.

"Okay, now how do I appease it?" Wayne asked Josie directly with certainty that she knew.

"How should I know? They didn't have cell phones when I was last up here." Josie quipped. "Maybe you should rub it."

Wayne gave her a very shocked look. "I'm not going to rub a tower to please it."

"It could be like a genie lamp. You have to rub it to get the person inside who will grant you the use of your phone to come out." Josie's voice had such certainty to it and that puzzled Wayne.

"Okay, whatever. I'll rub the tower just to prove to you that it won't work." Wayne walked over to the tower and placed his hand on the cold metal leg and started to rub. "See, nothing."

The tower began to wiggle. Wayne jumped away and ran behind Josie but realized how not brave that looked he stepped out to her side, but still a little back. All the way up the tower from the legs to the tip it wiggled.

"Told you so." Josie smiled.

Wayne just watched in shock. What on Earth was going on here? Then, his phone rang.

"Well, are you going to answer it?" Josie asked while staring at his pocket.

Wayne pulled out his phone and the caller ID just read: "Tower." He clicked the answer button and before he could talk a deep voice boomed out through the speaker.

"Ah! You must be the new Master of the Estate. Welcome!"

"Umm, who is this?" Wayne asked.

"Can you read?"

"Yes."

"Your fat and fleshy brain is so slow. I am the tower."

Wayne looked up at the Tower. He didn't see a face or a mouth anywhere, let alone any indication the Tower was alive.

"I assume you're here about your cell service. Am I right?"

"Yes. I was told…"

"Great! All you have to do is open up your phone, take out the SIM card, and eat it."

Wayne and Josie both looked up at the Tower with one of those you cannot be serious looks on their faces.

"Are you kidding?" Wayne asked.

"No, of course not. Look at your phone. Do you have service?"

"No."

"Yet I was able to call you. Clearly I have some way of doing that and therefore you should trust me when I tell you that you need to eat your SIM card in order for you to make phone calls while on this property." The Tower said assertively.

Josie nodded, pulled out her phone, took out the SIM card and ate it.

"What did you just do?" Wayne screamed.

Josie looked at her phone and the service bars ticked up from zero to full. "Oh neat! Look!" She showed her phone to Wayne.

"No. No way am I eating a piece of plastic. A piece of plastic with a computer chip inside. Sorry, but you guys can play your games with someone else. I'm outta here." He hung up on the Tower and went back to the hatch.

"Wayne, wait!" Josie chased him. "It's not a joke."

"Josie, you seem really sweet and I can get hazing the new guy but eating your SIM card…that's very dangerous. And I'm not Mr. Danger." He climbed down into the shaft and headed back into the house.

Chapter 8

Wayne shoved his shirts into his backpack. They had been folded neatly and put away by Morese, but now they were back to their natural state in a crumpled ball. He threw one strap over his shoulder and hurried out the door.

Outside the mansion he looked around for his car. It was nowhere to be seen. He ran back inside where Josie was slowly making her way down the stairs from the armoire.

"Where are you going?" She asked with her head hung low.

Wayne ignored the question and rushed over to the panel of call buttons on the entry hall wall. He scanned across the names but wasn't sure who to call so he flattened his hand and pressed them all.

"Wayne, please don't go." Josie was about to cry. "I haven't had a friend in such a long time."

Morese showed up first from behind Wayne, startling him. Ginger strode in next followed by Santiago. Based on the earlier interaction, Wayne assumed O'Connor would not be joining them.

"Is there a problem Mr. Morris?" Morese stepped toward the frantic Wayne. Wayne didn't speak, but not for lack of trying. He simply stomped because he was so frustrated that he could not form a single word.

"This better be good!" O'Connor blasted in tracking mud with his boots and holding a shovel in one hand. "I was in the middle of something very important in the swamps." He slammed the shovel hard down into the rug splitting the fibers and scarring the wood beneath.

Wayne nearly fell but was caught by Santiago. "Mi amigo. I only have one leg and I can stand up better than you." Santiago charmed, with Wayne in a comforting embrace. Wayne shook his way out of it and scrambled across the floor.

"If you wanted a peak you should have just asked." Ginger flirted with the clueless Wayne who was nearly under her dress.

Wayne shot up and stood surrounded by the Fairweather Estate staff and Josie. He looked at each one who all had a gaze of concern painted on their face.

"Listen," Wayne finally spoke up, "I don't know why Mrs. Fairweather gave all this to me, but it is far too weird for my taste. I mean, that's a human head!" Wayne pointed to a shrunken head in a glass case near the door. "You all seem nice. Weird, but nice. This just isn't me. I'm boring. That's my job. People will probably tell me I'm crazy for giving up a mansion and what must be at least twenty acres of land."

"Oh, it's much more than that." O'Connor chimed in.

"Regardless, I was happy in my crappy little apartment eating cold pizza and drinking cheap beer. I was comfortable with the fact that the only adventures I went on were digital. I could work my entire life and never achieve this amount of money, but I think I'm okay with that. If being rich means living with a talking cell phone tower who is trying to convince me to eat my SIM card just so I can make a phone call, count me out." Wayne finished his speech while looking at Josie. "I'm sorry I can't be the friend you wanted. You should probably go see a doctor."

Wayne started out the door. "Whoever is in charge of parking cars can you bring mine around?"

"At once, Sir." Morese bowed as he made his exit.

"I'm not your...whatever." Wayne walked out the main doors and down the front steps.

"Can I get back to my work now? The amount of time I have wasted could yield very hazardous results." O'Conner accepted the silence of the room as approval and removed the shovel and followed Wayne out.

"I'm sorry, Sugar. I know how long you've waited for someone your age to move in again. Lord knows I have too. For you. Keep your head up, Doll." Ginger rubbed Josie's shoulder then left her alone.

Tears ran down Josie's face and dropped to the floor. Her phone began to ring. She pulled it out of her pocket and her eyes grew wide at the name on the screen.

Wayne kicked the dirt as Morese pulled his car around. Josie ran out as Morese handed Wayne his keys.

"Wait!" Josie yelled. "Wayne! My phone!"

"What?" Wayne watched Josie running toward him and turned to Morese, but he was already gone. "I won't miss that."

"Wayne!" Josie reached Wayne and held her phone out to him. "It's for you."

"I don't need your phone Josie. Mine will work fine as soon as I leave this place."

"No, there's someone on the phone for you." She shook the phone in his face until he took it from her.

"Who would call me on your phone?" Wayne put the phone to his ear with hesitation. "Hello?"

"Young man! You are not going to throw this away because of some tiny piece of plastic, are you? You made me a promise." The voice of an old woman yelled through the phone's speaker.

"Mrs. Fairweather?"

Chapter 9

The world spun around Wayne as if he were in a Michael Bay movie with Martin Lawrence saying, "S**t just got real." Josie, on the other end of the shock spectrum, had a smile you could see from space and her tears had completely dried from her cheeks.

"Listen, this is a sick joke. I watched Mrs. Fairweather die. I already told you I was done with this place. Don't bring a dead woman into this." Wayne scolded the person on the other end of the line.

"It's my soul I can drag it wherever I please." Mrs. Fairweather scolded back.

"Is it really you?"

"You would think that stepping one foot into my house would make you accept this sort of possibility."

"When you told me to live my life, I didn't know you meant eating electronics, living wall decorations, and talking to dead people on the phone."

"What did you think I meant? Take a road trip to Portland and try the organic coffee?"

Wayne locked eyes with Josie. It only took a second for her to believe this was really Mrs. Fairweather on the phone. Did eating her SIM card really open a direct line with the dead?

"You promised me, and I gave you the means to go on whatever adventure you please and even on some you might not want at first, but isn't that what adventure is about?

Stepping out of your comfort zone and seeing what you're really made of?"

Wayne looked at his beat-up old car and thought about his life back home. His apartment was a mess. The chair he spent the majority of his time in was molding with spilt beer and he was pretty sure he didn't even shut his front door all the way when he left so there likely wasn't even a TV or computer left to digitally escape through anyway.

"If this is really Mrs. Fairweather, answer me one question."

"Anything, Sweetheart. I got the answer."

"What kind of pudding did you have in the hospital?"

"What is with you and pudding? It is like you're obsessed with it. It was tapioca and if I recall I did not even get a chance to eat it. Did you take it home?"

Wayne smiled. He couldn't believe he was talking to a dead person and for some reason it didn't scare him. "No, I would never take a dead woman's pudding."

"Now, back to the matter at hand Mr. Changes the subject." Mrs. Fairweather changed the subject. "I remembered the pudding. Do you remember your promise?"

"Yes." Wayne took a moment and looked at Josie. She was so happy, and her happiness made her even prettier than before. "I'll stay." Josie jumped and grabbed him. She almost took him to the ground, but Wayne caught their fall by latching onto his car. He got Josie back to a stable and standing position and continued his conversation with Mrs. Fairweather. "However, I have one condition."

"Okay. What is it?" Mrs. Fairweather asked with a tone that didn't portray much enthusiasm.

"If things get too weird or dangerous, I'm out."

"That's all?" Mrs. Fairweather laughed. "Don't worry, we have plenty of ways to keep you safe. Now, take that pretty girl, get on the roof, and eat that darn computer chip!"

"Thank you, Mrs. Fairweather."

"Don't thank me. Thank Josie. I wouldn't have been able to talk to you if she hadn't taken a leap of faith and done what you couldn't. Take care of her."

"I will."

"Goodbye now. You won't be hearing from me for a while."

"Why not? Why can't you just call?"

"If the dead were just allowed to call the living willy nilly the world would be in chaos. Trust me, you don't want that. Be well."

"Goodbye Mrs. Fairweather." Wayne pulled the phone away from his ear and all that was left was static hissing through the line.

"Thank you for staying, Wayne." Josie blushed.

"Come on. I have an inedible object to ingest."

Wayne and Josie stood before the Tower.

"You're back." The Tower boasted. "Finally, ready to trust me?"

"Something like that." Wayne said. He took the SIM card out of his phone and looked at Josie. "Did it hurt going down?" He asked her.

"It's like eating a chip and not chewing it all the way and a sharp corner goes down wrong." Josie said with excitement.

"Well, yippie." Wayne said with zero excitement. Down the hatch."

"No! You can't back out again!" Josie stood between him and the hatch to the ladder shaft.

Wayne paused with the SIM card dangling above his mouth and realized what she thought he was saying.

"No, I'm not leaving. It's a saying." Wayne assured her.

"Good. I don't know if I can get any more dead people to call you."

Wayne placed the SIM card slowly on his tongue, closed his mouth, and waited a moment then swallowed. The card ripped down his throat and got stuck for a moment, but before he knew it the SIM card made its way down.

"You're right. It did feel like a rogue chip piece."

"Isn't it great?"

"No, not at all."

Wayne looked at his phone and watched the service boost up to full.

"Now I can connect you to anyone from anywhere in the universe." The Tower explained through Wayne's phone. "However, the further you are from me the faster your battery will drain, so make use of this gift wisely."

Wayne looked at his phone, puzzled. "Don't worry. I don't think I'll be visiting Mars anytime soon."

He smiled and took Josie's hand then walked her over to the edge of the roof. They looked out across the estate. Small clearings could be seen through trees, some areas looked like they were experiencing different seasons than others while some had large structures poking out above the canopy.

"Okay, I've had enough heights for one day." Wayne backed away from the edge.

The two new friends walked back to the hatch together and as Wayne helped Josie onto the ladder both their phones started to ring. Wayne answered his.

"Hey Boyo. You pack your rain gear? I got a little matter I could use your assistance with." O'Connor barked.

Wayne looked at Josie who was listening in on her phone. Her eyes were wide with excitement. "Sure, why not?"

Chapter 10

"I've never owned a pair of boots. The moment I'm given nice ones, I take them to the swamp and get them covered in mud." Wayne complained with privilege.

"I don't think this is mud." Josie added.

The vastness of his estate was made clear to him by the twenty-minute drive to the outskirts of the swamplands. Swamps like this aren't regulars to Oklahoma. He had only seen swamps like this on reality television with shows like "Alligator Baiters" and "Bayou Treasure." Two particularly good shows that are perfect for just having something on. One of the guys from "Alligator Baiters" lost his arm to a gator last season when he reached into the gator's mouth for a crowd of fifty people. Way more than that if you count their television audience. Wayne wondered for a moment if he'd be back this season.

The trees were slimy with moss and the water stank of stagnation. Every step filled Wayne's boots with a healthy portion of gunk adding at least a half a pound each time. Wayne hadn't done this much exercise since Middle School P. E. This trek right after scaling the ladder to the roof of his new home had him so worn out, he was becoming delirious. He didn't dare mention it to Josie, but his tired mind had him believing the ground under the muck was moving.

"You doing okay back there?" Josie hollered while making pace at least ten feet in front.

"Oh, I'm just grand. A million bucks as a matter of fact." Wayne put on a show. "As a matter of fact, I bet you the West Wing of the house you can't get to O'Connor before me." Wayne immediately regretted saying that as he knew he was making the best time he could.

"The West Wing is nothing but servants' quarters and storage of old maps." Josie retorted. "Nice try there, speed demon."

Wayne nearly fainted with relief. Not that he really cared all that much about square footage, it was that he really didn't want to have to pretend to race. If he was going to be going on any more adventures with Josie, he was going to need to install a gym at the house or at least find out if one already existed. However, from what little bizarreness he already knew of the house, he felt it would be wise to be weary of an existing facility.

Josie charged ahead. Her steps didn't seem to sink into the putrid puddles of gunk as much as Wayne's did. As a matter of fact, she seemed to float on top. Wayne figured it was just the fumes seeping into his every pore that was causing him to hallucinate. "Look up ahead!" Josie shouted. "I think I see O'Connor."

Wayne focused his eyes on the location Josie was pointing to. He could barely see the rugged man in the distance, and he appeared to be frantically filling in a hole on what Wayne hoped was more solid land.

Sweat and mud-covered O'Connor's face and body. He spotted his two helpers coming up through the half sunken trees. "Grab a shovel lads." O'Connor directed their attention to a cart of garden tools using his head. "We need to get these holes filled in before it wakes up."

Josie rushed over to the cart and immediately began filling in a nearby hole. Wayne stopped dead in his tracks and looked at the ground.

"What do you mean, 'It?'"

"No time to chat about what 'It' is or isn't or could become. You won't get a chance to understand it if we don't fill in these damn holes." O'Connor urged while he continued to scoop load after load of mud and dirt into the holes.

"Hurry, Wayne! Grab a shovel!" Josie matched O'Connor's intensity blindly.

Wayne sucked up his fear and headed over to the cart. He reached in and grabbed a shovel and before he could turn to the others to find a hole to fill, the ground rumbled like a hungry stomach. "What was that? An earthquake?" Wayne shuttered.

"No, Lad. That was 'It'" O'Connor quipped.

The three of them went to work scooping and shoveling. There must have been at least ten more holes to fill when the second rumble hit.

"I'm assuming this, whatever, lives under the ground and that these holes lead to its lair or dungeon or whatever." Josie's voice was filled with panic. "I mean, if you knew about 'It' then why didn't you take care of this soonerrrrrr!" Josie's leg was gripped by a slimy, strong, and thick tentacle and she was pulled to the ground.

"Josie!" Wayne screamed, but didn't move.

Josie plunged her shovel into the ground for leverage, but the creature was too strong and pulled her screaming into the hole. O'Connor ran to the hole and started filling it in.

"What are you doing!" Wayne finally ran over and tried to stop O'Connor. "You're going to trap her in there!"

"Exactly!" O'Connor shook Wayne off and continued. "And to answer her question, we weren't expecting 'It' for another three years. Now hurry up and help me. If we fill in the rest of the holes that will force it to surface in the hole of our choosing and we might just have a chance to save your little girlfriend."

"She's not my girlfriend." Wayne spoke bluntly.

"Who bloody cares? Get to work!"

Wayne and O'Connor tripled their hole filling speed as other tentacles shot up from various other exits. Each time a tentacle made an appearance, Wayne and O'Connor made that hole their next target. Hole after hole they filled them in until they came to the last one.

"Now what?" Wayne managed to say between deep breaths of fatigue.

"Now we wait for the dance." O'Connor just barely finished his sentence when a tentacle shot straight up, and he hacked it in half with his spade. The severed limb flopped to the ground and thrashed about. "Comm'on boy. I'm not going to get that lucky with every strike. Going ta need your blade."

"I... I..." Wayne froze.

"There are twelve more of those bastards and one of them has taken a deep liking to Miss. Josie. Are you going to just stand there blubbering..." A tentacle wiggled out along the ground. O'Connor jumped and dodged it while piercing it to the ground. "...like an idiot?" O'Connor held strong as the tentacle tried to retract and ultimately ripped itself in two. "Or are you going to help?" O'Connor sent a harsh glance at Wayne's direction, but Wayne still did nothing. "Sweet Mother of the Lake. You're a true coward."

O'Connor grabbed Wayne's shovel and dual welded them like a knife and dinner fork, stabbing and cutting his way through the remaining tentacles. Nearly dead himself from exhaustion O'Connor said a prayer. "Our Lord of the sky and light. Father of the moon and keeper of time. Give me the strength to carry out your will and end this abomination."

The final tentacle with Josie in its grip emerged and stretched high into the air. Josie screamed the entire time. The creature was wild and agitated. It spun and crashed through nearby trees. Its oozing flesh passed inches above Wayne's head, but he still didn't move. O'Connor jumped back three feet as it made an attack on him and just before it was to strike he sent both shovels down and deep through its soft and wet skin. Josie fell to the ground still wrapped up in a dead grasp. O'Connor pulled out one of the shovels and scooped it in under Josie's butt and popped her out like a pimple. She rolled away and O'Connor went to work filling in the last hole.

Wayne snapped out of his daze and noticed Josie lying on the ground. He ran over to her.

"Josie! Are you okay?" He held her tightly.

Josie opened her eyes slowly and they grew wider and wider as did her smile. "Are you kidding me?"

"I'm so sorry."

"I'm great!" Josie leaped up and began to dance around the swampy ground. "That was incredible! I was pulled through tunnel after tunnel and then shot up into the sky." She acted out every motion as she spoke them. "And then..." She looked at Wayne. "Oh my God! You saved me!" She ran back over to Wayne and wrapped him tighter in her arms than the creature had done to her. "Thank you, thank you, thank you! My hero!"

Wayne just laughed and let her hug away. O'Connor patted down the last of the hole covering and cleared his throat while glaring coldly at Wayne. Wayne pried himself free, "Actually, Josie. I sort of froze."

Josie's gaze was blank, but her smile remained. "Froze?"

"Yeah, O'Connor was the one. He did everything. He's your hero." Wayne said painfully.

"Oh." Josie's smile disappeared. She turned to O'Conner, stretched out her arm and shook his hand. "Thank you, Sir. I owe you my life."

"Nonsense, Lass. You'd've done the same for me." O'Connor released her hand and started toward the tool cart. "Now, let's get home. I could go for one of Santiago's famous grilled cheese sandwiches."

Josie gave one even sadder look at Wayne then sulked off after O'Connor. Wayne's heart contorted and he felt as if the now dead creature's grip had him and that he was going to die as he watched Josie leave.

The swamp monster battling team arrived back at the house and Josie headed off for her home. O'Connor grabbed Wayne by the arm as he was heading up the front steps.

"Boyo, you better brave up. I might not be there next time and you're gonna lose that girl."

"I think I already did."

"Nonsense. If there is one thing I know, it's women. She'll forgive you. You just need to give her a reason to." O'Connor picked up the handles of his tool cart and shuffled off.

"Good on ya for coming clean though." O'Connor hollered without looking back. "That's something at least."

Wayne pulled out his phone to call Josie and noticed that he had a missed call from his regular client, Mark.

Morese came out of the house and placed a long towel on the ground for Wayne to remove his disgusting boots on. He helped balance Wayne as he pulled off the likely ruined footwear. Wayne just stared at his phone and the voicemail notification from Mark.

"Morese. Pull my car around, please. I have something boring to do."

Chapter 11

The exposed foundation showed signs of movement in the earth below. Long cracks splintered across the living room giving a clear sign that it was time to consider getting piers installed in his house.

Wayne wasn't sure what Mark did for a living, but he clearly had enough money that he didn't need to be at work at two o'clock on a Wednesday and could pay Wayne's fifteen dollar an hour rate. Mark also wasn't really the type to be all that concerned with such structural issues and was clearly more interested in how the place looked on the surface. It would have to be a visible crack down a wall for him to put effort into fixing the problem. However, he might just buy a giant painting to cover it up if it came to that.

The contractors were hauling in long rolls of padding when Wayne arrived. Scraps of soft material smashed and fused together to give a nice comfortable layer between the new carpet and the slab. The mundane aspect of watching these three men install carpet in Mark's house was exactly what Wayne needed after the events in the swamp.

"Wayne! My man!" Mark stood up from his lawn chair and greeted Wayne as he came through the sliding glass doorway to the backyard. "Grab a brew and a seat."

"Good to see you Mark." Wayne opened the lid to the thick blue plastic cooler that sat next to Mark's carpet installation spectator section.

"Good to see you Mark." Mark mocked Wayne's very professional speech pattern. "Could I interest you in a life insurance policy from MetLife?"

"Sorry. I haven't been myself lately." Wayne took a seat and cracked his beer.

"Spill it brother. I'm all ears."

"I'd rather not get into it. Besides, you wouldn't believe me if I told you."

"Okay. No pressure."

Mark and Wayne sat in silence for at least a minute. The contractors started to roll out the padding and cut it to fit the shape of the room.

"Why are we watching them install your new carpet?" Wayne finally spoke up. "Are you afraid they'll steal something?"

"No, man. I just figured it would be a good excuse to give my buddy Wayne a call for a beer and a chill session."

"Well, now I feel bad for charging you."

"What else would I do with my money? Go see a movie and get fat on popcorn?" Mark patted his stomach. "I'd rather get fat on beer in the comfort of my own home."

"Do you mind if I ask you a personal question?" Wayne nervously asked.

"Of course not, man. Dig in."

"You're single right?"

"Hey man, if this is going where I think it's going, I'm gonna need to stop you right there. I'm flattered, but that's not what I'm looking for with you."

"Oh no! I asked because I'm sort of having trouble with a girl."

"Man! I knew something was getting you down the last time we hung. What's the deal? She know you like her? She doesn't know? She does know, but doesn't like you? She cheat on you? Do I need to kill her?"

"No. None of those. Well maybe one, but that's not the problem." Wayne paused and took a drink. "She thinks I'm a coward."

"Why would she think that?"

"That's sort of the part of the story you won't believe."

"Try me."

"Okay, but I warned you."

Wayne went into the whole story with Mark from the moment he got his first visit from the Suit Man. Mark's attention wavered at times from really interested to skeptical. Wayne wasn't much of a storyteller, so his version of the events often fell a little flat and often out of order.

"So, let me get this right. The swamp is a metaphor for a bar and the monster was a dude who wouldn't leave her alone, but you didn't do anything to help her get out of it." Mark wrapped it up in a way that made sense to himself.

"Sure."

"Man, you're quite the storyteller. Usually it's just the 'So I have this friend right...' storyline." Mark remarked. "I'll tell you what I know. Women tend to have way too high of expectations. They want the big house, nice cars, champion show dogs, for you to save their lives, crap like that. Not to mention love."

Wayne spit up his beer at the mention of love. "Oh, no. I don't love her."

"Man, you wouldn't be such a mess about her if you didn't." This was the most serious Mark had been the entire time they'd ever spent together.

"We just met. Trust me. She thinks of me as a friend and that's it."

"You might not love her, but she might just love you. Would explain her attitude about your actions." Mark cracked another beer. The sound echoed through the half-carpeted house. It made the contractor's stop for a moment and stare at the cooler with lust in their eyes. "Either that or she just gets really cranky when she almost dies."

Wayne thought about what Mark was saying and decided to change the subject to a conversation that was less heavy. They discussed standard guy stuff like sports, TV, and music and before too long and before too many beers that aimed to prevent Wayne from being able to drive home, the contractors were finished and Mark pulled out his wallet to pay. Wayne refused to take his money, this time knowing he had a fortune waiting for him back at the house.

"At least let me give you a tip for bringing an element of storytelling into the mix. It was like hangouts and a show." Mark handed Wayne a twenty. "I insist."

Wayne took Mark's money but realized that Mark didn't really consider what he told him about the swamp and Josie to be real and that it was likely no one in the rest of the world would. He got in his car, clipped on the seatbelt, and drove home feeling very disconnected from life.

Chapter 12

The smell of fresh baked ham hit Wayne's nose the moment he walked in the door. He had always been a sucker for a spiral cut honey ham. Wayne followed the scent through the air and imagined himself floating and being pulled in by the scent just like Shaggy and Scooby from TV. Dodging doorways and chairs, Wayne's nose brought him to the kitchen where the makings of a feast were in the middle of preparation. The amount of food Wayne saw must have taken an army of chefs to produce, but he looked around and saw nobody. Not even Santiago. On the counter in front of him was the ham glowing with sweet savory wonder. It was cut and the edges peeled and folded over each other in a waterfall of ham heaven. Since the house was his then the ham must be his too. Wayne was starting to see the perks of being a millionaire of a strange home, but not all of them. He made his way over and reached for his prize to grab just a tiny bite. His fingers came within mere centimeters of the ham when a loud whack from across the room made Wayne slip and fall to the ground.

"I am deeply sorry, Senór. You cannot eat that now." Santiago pulled a large cleaver from the cutting board in front of him. "If you are hungry now, I will gladly whip you up something, but all of this is not to be touched."

Wayne pulled himself up front the ground. "I really need to learn how to stand up better." He brushed his clothes with his hands as if dusting himself off, but in doing so realized it was just a strange habit and there wasn't anything to dust off.

Santiago's kitchen was incredibly spotless for having produced so much food. Around the ham were platters of fruit and vegetables arranged like great islands of healthiness. Bacon wrapped jalapeno poppers were in the stove and trays with various shapes and types of crackers with deli meats and exotic cheese were stacked around the perimeter. Pizza, sliders, and tacos as far as the eye could see. French fries and nachos covered in melted cheese. This was like Wayne's idea of heaven. He began to panic a little bit fearing that maybe he had died in the swamp and that's why he froze. However, this couldn't be heaven because in heaven he'd be able to eat the food. "Is this hell?" Wayne screamed.

"Oh dear. I usually have a gift for knowing exactly the pallet of someone and can craft a menu of all their favorite foods, but I must be getting sloppy." The panic spread to Santiago.

"What do you mean? This all looks amazing, but if I can't eat it then I must be in hell."

Santiago let out a great sigh of relief and started to laugh uncontrollably. "You are not in hell, Senór. Nor have you died at all." Santiago explained mid laugh while also flinging his cleaver around. "This food is all for your housewarming party tonight."

"Housewarming party?" Wayne didn't remember anyone telling him about a housewarming party.

"Why of course! You are the new master of the estate. There must be a party in your honor."

"I haven't invited anyone."

"All the arrangements have been taken care of by Mrs. Fairweather's attorney." Santiago pulled a bowl from under the counter then walked over to the stove where a pot of chili was simmering. "Or should I say, your attorney." He scooped a healthy portion of chili into the bowl and topped it with corn chips, relish, and cheese. "Here, since I gave you such a fright you may have a bowl of Frito Chili Pie. Just like your mom used to make." Santiago handed Wayne the bowl.

Wayne sat down on a stool and stared at the chili. "I don't deserve Frito Chili Pie. I don't deserve a party." He set the bowl aside. "I'm no master. I'm nothing but a coward."

Santiago was cutting up a batch of carrots in rapid succession. The knife brushed his knuckles with every chop. One false move and the large stainless-steel blade would slice through his fingers like butter. Without missing a beat, he took his eyes off the carrots and onto Wayne. "Did something happen in the swamp?"

"You could say that."

"Tell me about it." Santiago grabbed carrot after carrot, chopping them up like it was second nature.

"Long story short, Josie was in danger and I did nothing to save her." Wayne hung his head and using his fork he pushed the corn chips around the top of the chili as if they were surfboards and his fork was a tall surfer with three legs, no arms, and big round butt.

Santiago's chopping stopped. "Is she still in danger?" Santiago moved closer to him. "Did you leave her out there?" The knife in his hands was no longer a threat to the shape of the carrots and was now pointed directly at Wayne. "Tell me what you did!" Santiago screamed.

Wayne whipped up the fork in defense. "Nothing!" He panicked. "I mean, she's okay. O'Connor saved her."

Santiago smiled and lowered the knife. "Ah, well at least we know you value your own life." Santiago pointed with his knife to Wayne's fork. "Now put that thing down before you get startled again and poke an eye out." He went back to his carrots and picked right up where he left off. "So, you froze, and she's upset with you?"

"Pretty much. I don't know what to do."

"Have you tried talking to her about it? I mean, after she's had time to think it through."

Wayne realized he didn't end up calling her like he had planned and ran off to the real world instead. "No, I should do that now, huh?" He jumped off the stool and pulled out his phone and began to look for her number. A carrot zoomed through the air and knocked the phone from his hands.

"No." Santiago had thrown the carrot without missing a second of chopping. "You need to know what it is you are apologizing for before you go throwing around the words, 'Lo siento.'"

"Huh?"

"I'm sorry."

"You should be. That hurt!"

"That's Spanish for 'I'm sorry.'"

"Oh. My bad. I mean, lo siento." Wayne picked up his phone and brushed off water from the freshly washed carrot that it had connected with his face. "I know what I'm sorry for. I did nothing to save her."

"But why? Until you truly know what it means to protect, you will never know what it means to save." Santiago brushed all the chopped carrots into a container, wiped off his blade on his apron, and walked over to a counter where a notepad sat. "You need to go on a quest."

"A quest?" Wayne walked closer to Santiago hesitantly. He was still a bit nervous that he would throw more produce at him. "Is that different from an adventure?"

"Mucho. On an adventure you seek a prize. On a quest, you seek yourself." Santiago scribbled something down on the notepad and ripped off the top sheet. "You must participate in the Trial of Errands." Santiago handed Wayne the piece of paper. Wayne looked at the paper. It read, 'Fetch a dozen coocoo berries.'

"I don't get it."

"I cannot tell you what it means. You must figure it out for yourself." Santiago turned and went back to work. He poured the chopped carrots into a large pot of water and began to bring them to a boil. "Other members of the estate will have similar tasks for you to complete. After you have completed these tasks, you will know what to say to Miss Josie. Now go."

Wayne left the kitchen not looking where he was going. His eyes were fixed on the paper Santiago had given him and what Fetch a dozen coocoo berries meant. He made it all the way into the entry hall repeating the phrase, "Fetch a dozen coocoo berries, fetch a dozen coocoo berries, a dozen coocoo berries, a dozen coocoo…" He stopped dead in his tracks and laughed to himself. "You dumb idiot, Wayne." He folded the paper and put it in his pocket and opened the front door. "A dozen coocoo berries." His laughter at his own stupidity was very funny to him. "Eggs. A dozen coocoo berries are eggs."

Chapter 13

The air outside had that cool pre rain feeling. Wind rushed across the estate and with it brought a fresh clean smell of the coming storm. Wayne closed his eyes and took in the sensation. His hair tossed around, and he stretched his arms out. The paper with Santiago's request flapped wildly in the wind and Wayne tried picturing what Josie would have been thinking. The whipping and ripping of the paper gave off a vibrating and popping sound that Wayne likened to the engine of an airplane. He was now flying. His plane was light like a World War I fighter. With every irregularity in the wind's gust Wayne imagined he was dipping and diving through the clouds. He smiled, but this feeling of freedom unlocked by his own mind made him sad and he remembered what he'd not done for Josie. Thunder shook him from his daydream, and he decided he probably should find his car to make the long trip down the driveway to Miss Sally's.

Wayne ran up the front steps and back inside to ring Morese. Santiago met him at the call buttons in the entry hall and slapped his knife over the brass knobs.

"Forgive me. I forgot to tell you that I will need you to complete this task on foot." Santiago explained.

"But it's about to rain. Why can't I just drive." Wayne was confused.

"It's called the Trial of Errands." Santiago said plainly. "It wouldn't be much of a trial if it was easy." Wayne let out a long sigh and turned back out the front doors. "Don't worry. A little bit water never killed anyone. A whole lot. Sometimes. Don't worry about that. It's rain. You'll dry."

Wayne stepped outside and looked up at the clouds. They were beginning to turn the type of scary dark that Oklahomans got excited about due to the prospect of tornados. Wayne wasn't like that. He knew the real dangers a storm could have and preferred to stay inside and safe during them. His hand was gripped tight around Santiago's note and Josie's laugh raced through his mind. With all the will power in his body, Wayne forced his legs to move and he set off with a pace of an Olympic speed walker, but with much worse form.

He could see lightning in the distance and used an old Cub Scout trick he'd learned as a way of counting the seconds between the flash and when you hear the thunder to determine how far away the storm was. His body still in a goofy speed walk shuffle he tried counting. "One. Two. Three. Four…" He started to feel a bit of relief that it was a bit of a way away. "…Five. Six. Seven. Eight…" Eight miles was forever away. His pace slowed down, but he continued counting. "Nine. Ten…" Boom! The thunder rolled out and shook the sky and Wayne's heart. He panicked for a second but thought if eight miles was okay then ten is even better. Santiago was right after all. A little bit of rain wasn't going to kill him. "Right?"

Wayne was now walking at a regular pace. He looked around the thick tree lined driveway and noticed the cemetery up ahead he'd seen the first time he drove up. Seeing the tombstones wasn't the best imagery to come along after assuring himself he wasn't going to die. Right as he came to the edge of the cemetery, he held his breath for good luck. Another flash of lightning and Wayne started his count again. This time in his head. One. Two. Three. Four. Five. Six. Boom! Wayne jumped and let out his breath and noticed he hadn't made it all the way past the cemetery yet. So much for good luck. The storm had moved four miles in just a matter of minutes.

Wayne's casual walk jumped way past speed walk and into full on run.

Lightning struck. Wayne counted. One. Two. Three. Boom! He tried desperately to increase his pace, but unfortunately, he'd spent more time picking out what toppings he wanted on his pizzas than on a treadmill. Up ahead he could see the trees thinning out and knew he was about to the end of the drive, which meant Miss Sally's was close. Flash. One. Two. Boom! Wayne started to sweat. Flash. One. Boom! He felt like closing his eyes, but knew that would probably not be the best idea considering he was running at a speed that he hadn't ran at since he was eleven on a road he was just getting to know. Flash. Boom! Wayne banked the turn and sprinted to Miss Sally's door. He could hear the trees nearby getting beat with rain. He grabbed the handle and pulled, but it didn't open. Wayne stopped, looked inside, and Miss Sally's was closed.

"You have got to be kidding me!" Wayne looked up to see how much overhang he had under the awning. What stared back was the narrowest lip of iron and fabric he had ever seen. The clearance wasn't any more than a couple inches. The rain was coming closer and he could see where it had started to hit the road. It moved like a perfect wall toward him. Wayne's first and only thought was that he needed to find something to break the window with to get inside. Afterall he was rich now and he could easily pay Miss Sally or whoever it was that owned the shop back. This very well could be a life and death situation. Maybe. His eye shot over to his right to a half of a brick. That was too small. To the left he spotted a road work sign propped up on the side of the building. It was made of metal and thick wood. This was perfect. He grabbed it and drug it over to the front of the store. His eyes met the rain wall that was inching closer and closer and he let out a tiny laugh and got to work. The sign was heavy, but Wayne pulled together everything he had and picked it up and went in for the swing when headlights flashed and an old brown Oldsmobile with a torn fabric top pulled up and parked.

A woman, with frizzy grey hair and a bad blonde dye job that she must have gotten a couple years ago, got out and ran over to the door. "I am so sorry I'm late." She pulled out a set of keys and began to unlock the door not even noticing that Wayne was holding the sign he was intending to use to smash the door down. "My car was giving me trouble again." The door opened and the woman held it for Wayne. The rain was almost upon them, so he just pushed the sign over into the parking lot and ran inside followed by the woman. "You must be the new young man who took over Mrs. Fairweather's estate. I'm Sally Sugarman. This is my husband's place." Sally offered her delicate hand to Wayne for him to kiss instead of shake. He awkwardly leaned down and gave her wrinkled skin a peck. She pulled her hand back and went behind the counter and flipped on the lights.

The rain splashed the road sign outside and Wayne started to calm down a bit. Just as his heart slowed to a regular pace a bolt of lightning struck the sign creating a captivating flash. Wayne stood in horror staring at what could have been his end. "Did you say your husband owns the place?"

"That's right." Sally put on a name tag that said Sally. "He's owned it ever since we got ourselves married forty years ago."

"Then why is it called 'Miss Sally's.'"

"I don't understand your question."

"Never mind. Do you have eggs here?"

"You mean coocoo berries? Of course. Got some fresh in the trunk." Sally came out from behind the counter and walked past Wayne and grabbed an umbrella. "I picked them fresh from the bush this morning." She chuckled and went outside to her car.

"That's a visual I'll never forget." Wayne watched Sally pull a box from her trunk and shut the lid all while staying calm, cool, and dry under the umbrella. Made him feel extremely manly.

Sally came back in and set the umbrella aside to dry out and brought the eggs over to the counter. "How many do you need, dear?"

"Twelve. Thank you."

Sally pulled one carton out of the box and handed them to Wayne. The carton was a little old and Wayne could tell it had been reused. "Came from my best coop this morning. Lots of protein." Sally smiled and Wayne could see she was missing over half her teeth.

"How much do I owe you?" Wayne reached into his back pocket and discovered he didn't have his wallet. "And would you accept an I.O.U?"

"Oh, don't worry about it, dear. You can have em." Sally patted Wayne's hand on top of the egg carton. "That is if you will do me one favor."

Wayne smiled. Santiago did say there would be more than one errand in this Trial of Errands. "Is it safe?"

Sally puzzled her eyes in silence. Wayne's manhood was punched once again. He shook it off quickly. "What can I do?"

"Would you be a sweetheart take these roses and place them on my brother's grave on your way back?" Sally pulled out a bouquet of roses from the box. "He worked for the Fairweather's and is buried in the family plot."

Immediate regret struck Wayne. "Sure, it would be my pleasure."

"Oh, thank you!" Sally hopped a little. "We're about to get our rush and I just won't be able to get away. You're a lifesaver."

"Not quite."

"What was that?"

"Never mind. Do you get a lot of customers out here? You said rush. I can't imagine it getting too busy, especially with the rain."

"What rain?" Sally looked outside the front windows. Wayne followed suit. The rain had stopped, and a car was pulling up into the parking lot.

"Never mind that either." Wayne headed for the door. "It was nice to meet you Mrs., Miss...Sally." Wayne was met at the door by a tall man in coveralls.

"Sally, you know you got a street sign right in the middle of your parking spaces?" The Tall Man said in a very country accent.

"Oh dear. I wonder how that got there." Sally placed her hand over her heart as if it were a major shock to her system.

Wayne squeezed past the Tall Man and before he got completely out, he reached back in and looked at the umbrella. "Sally! Do you mind if I borrow your umbrella?" Wayne asked, involuntarily matching the accent of the Tall Man.

"Sure, though I don't see why you'd need it." Sally said.

"Just in case." Wayne grabbed the umbrella and pulled it through, but the opened top got stuck between the door and the body of the Tall Man. The Tall Man didn't move. "Excuse me." Wayne pushed the umbrella back into the store just enough to shut it and pulled it back through. As Wayne walked off past the windows, he watched the Tall Man waddle toward Sally while he played with the straps of his coveralls with his thumbs. He was the first-person Wayne had seen that fit the area since he came.

The roses and umbrella were gripped tight in Wayne's right hand while he cradled the carton of eggs like a baby with the left. Walking back up the driveway was a lot less stressful without the threat of possibly deadly rain and lightning since he had at least some form of protection in hand. Albeit one with a metal spike on top.

"Is this a golf umbrella?"

The graveyard wasn't too far down the drive. However, there wasn't much in the way of a marker, so he could judge distance. Strangely, the cemetery seemed to be as close to the house as it was Miss Sally's. Wayne knew for a fact that it took him longer to get from the cemetery to Miss Sally's than it did getting from Miss Sally's to the cemetery. The way back always seems faster, but not that fast. He had barely left the parking lot when he got to the cemetery. Where was that fold in space time when he was running from the storm, he thought?

There was a three-foot-high fence with barbed wire on top separating him and the tombstones. Wayne liked it that way because knowing this place, the likelihood of zombies increased tenfold and anything blocking their path to his brain was good with him. He couldn't see a gate into the little cemetery, so he figured he was going to have to climb over the barrier he loved so much. Unable to do that with his hands full, Wayne sat the eggs down and found a nice soft patch of clovers and nestled the carton in a sort of nest around them. Living on the second story of an apartment complex, Wayne had learned the hard way, multiple times, that eggs and their cartons are not very sturdy. He found a section of the fence that seemed to have fewer barbs where he could make his climb. Reaching through the lower rung of the fence with the roses he placed them safely on the other side and climbed over. From the top of the fence he jumped down and felt a slight pinch in his knees. Getting to the gym was going on his to-do list when he got home. First on that list was to make a to-do list.

He picked up the flowers and slowly crept through the graveyard examining the names on each tombstone as he went. There was Richard King born 1907 and died 1982. Under his name it read "He wrote. Period." Then there was Shelley Stein born 1797 and died 1851, "A real monster of a woman." Wayne continued along reading a few more names, Jacob Whocares, Tina Whatever, Elizabeth Somebody, and Mel Brooks. He stopped and doubled back to make sure he read the last one correctly. Leaning in he wiped some dirt from the first name to reveal it said Melanie Brooks. Wayne continued. He was looking for the name Anthony Arthur Avery.

As he searched, he passed a long line of Doyle's who all appeared to have died the same day then finally found Anthony's grave. Placing the flowers at the base of the tombstone Wayne read the inscription. Anthony Arthur Avery born 1942 and died 2001. "Died visiting his mother's grave." Wayne looked around and saw that the tombstone next to Arthur's belonged to an Agatha Avery. His eyes darted back to Arthur's grave and he reread the inscription. "Died visiting his mother's grave." Was that the real reason Sally had sent him to bring the roses? She knew something about this graveyard. She knew it was a dangerous place and she knew she'd rather sacrifice Wayne than risk dying herself.

"Free eggs my ass."

A noise at the tree line behind Arthur's grave caught Wayne's attention. Falling on his butt, he kicked rapidly at the dried leaves as he struggled to stand in a panic.

Russell, drag, snap, crackle, pop. The noises continued along the tree line. Wayne ducked behind Arthur's tombstone. "Sorry, Arty." Wayne whispered to Arthur's grave. The noises sounded like they were a few feet into the tree line and were moving away from Wayne. This was his chance to run. As his last sprint proved he wasn't completely confident in his running skills, but he just needed to make it about thirty feet and he'd be safe or at least safer with the fence between himself and whatever was there to kill him like it did poor Arthur. Wayne used his incredible public-school basic math skills to determine the noises were about thirty feet in the other direction and took his shot. He took off and didn't make it far before tripping on a flat headstone that wasn't calculated into his plan. Wayne fell hard, knocking the wind clear out of his chest. Instead of jumping back up he just remained there.

Maybe this was meant to be. He'd just lie there and die. No more worries. No more concerns that Josie thought he was a coward. No more dealing with the craziness of his new home. No more seeing Josie's crooked smile. No more awesome grilled cheeses. No more cookies from Josie. No more Josie. Wayne's plan to just die started feeling like a bad plan. He regained his breath and dug his hands into the dirt and pushed himself up, but that common body weight exercise was way too easy for the unathletic Wayne to perform especially after such a fall. His body felt like it was lifted by the sky. He felt his feet find their footing in the dirt and finally noticed the slight, but strong pull on the back of his shirt. All his waiting to live secured his death. The creature, or monster, or ghost, or giant freaking eagle had caught him and was preparing for the kill. Wayne closed his eyes and waited.

"What the damn hell are you doing 'ere, boyo?"

Wayne's eyes shot open and he turned around to see O'Connor.

"This ain't no place for the living."

"Oh man!" Wayne let out a long sigh of relief. "I thought you were a monster."

"Monster?" O'Connor looked at Wayne like he was stupid. "That beast in the swamp was a rare occurrence. Not every inch of this place has some kind of ghoul lurking around it." O'Connor explained.

"Then what killed Arthur?"

"Who's Arthur?"

"The man in that grave. With the roses." Wayne pointed to the freshly laid roses on Arthur's grave.

"That moron? He tripped over a headstone much like you just did, cept he didn't get as lucky as you and his face cracked open on a rock." O'Connor's stare put the fear of God in Wayne.

Wayne looked down at the ground and saw a stone near where he had landed, which had a slight red stain about it. "I was actually just leaving." He carefully turned and watched every step to make sure he didn't slip up and fall again.

"H'old it right there." O'Connor hollered. Wayne froze with one foot still in the air. He slowly moved it to the ground level and turned to O'Connor. "I need you to bring this to Morese for me." O'Connor walked over and handed Wayne a letter. "Found it on Mrs. Fairweather's grave."

Wayne took the letter and noticed the freshly filled in grave belonging to the wonderful woman who bequeathed him the estate. The sight of her burial plot gave Wayne a noticeably clear feeling that he should be leaving faster. He made it through the rest of the graveyard without falling and cracking his head open and soon was over the fence to retrieve his precious eggs. As if he were an archaeologist, Wayne brushed away the leaves and other soft covering he had used to protect the carton. The Styrofoam lid popped as he opened it to check and make sure all the eggs were still intact. Picking up each one individually, turning them and feeling their shells, Wayne determined that they were all in good health and continued the road back to the house.

The clouds above still held an air of storm in them. Thunder rolled faint in the distance, but Wayne was sure it was moving away from him based on the speed it had come in. He decided not to count this time and took the walk back with ease. Besides, he had the umbrella this time. The thunder bellowed a bit louder and Wayne wondered if there was a back half of the storm about to drop down. He gripped his right hand for the umbrella and discovered he wasn't holding it at all and stopped dead in his tracks and looked back down the road toward Miss Sally's. He must have forgotten to pick it back up when he grabbed the eggs. The thunder and lightning boomed and cracked followed by an almost immediate downpour of rain. Wayne burst into an all-out run cradling the carton of eggs like a football or at least how he'd seen athletes on TV cradle of a football. Up ahead he could see the house. His clothes were soaked, and his shoes squished with every step. He tried desperately to run faster, but he simply couldn't. The rain was hitting him hard in the face and he could barely see. Up ahead was a stone in the road and since his vision was so disturbed Wayne couldn't see it in time and stepped right on it, twisting his ankle sending him crashing to the ground. During his fall, time seemed to slow down, and he became painfully aware of the eggs in his care. Using every bit of strength in him he twisted his body midair and landed on his back keeping the eggs safe and sound on his chest. The breath had been knocked from his lungs and Wayne stared up at the fluffy grey storm clouds, which had graciously decided to stop their water onslaught just as Wayne fell.

Wayne pulled himself up by doing what was likely the first sit-up he had ever done in his entire life and stood, holding the carton of eggs in front of him. He popped the lid and checked each one carefully and upon discovering no cracks or damage he shut the lid and looked around to get his bearings. Turning back down the driveway to face the house resulted in a crisp cool breeze finding its way onto the crack of his butt via a rip in his pants. Perhaps eating all those chocolate chip cookies Josie brought him followed by Santiago's incredible grilled cheese wasn't the best choice of diet plan.

With the storm in a state of pause, Wayne saw Ginger in the courtyard pulling sheets of a clothesline quickly. He rushed over and set the eggs down in an almost full basket of sheets.

"Need some help?" Wayne offered.

"That is quite gentlemanly of you Master Wayne." Ginger glimmered a charming smile at her new employer. She continued to unclip sheets with speed and grace.

Wayne watched for a moment to study Ginger's technique and proceeded to do exactly as she did. As he unclipped and folded sheets he couldn't help, but glance over at Ginger. Something was different about her. Wayne knew it was rude to comment on a woman's looks unless it was all out flattery and, in this case, he believed what he wanted to ask fit this category. "Are you using some new makeup?" Wayne nervously asked. Ginger stopped cold. Her arms dropped from the sheet she was currently taking down and looked at Wayne. His heart sank. Surely, he just offended her. He was never good with words or talking to women and that isn't an extremely healthy combination for those few moments when he got the chance to.

"Why yes!" Ginger's southern draw squeaked out through a great big open mouth smile. Her wrinkles were far less prominent than the last time Wayne had seen her, and she overall looked ten years younger. "I can't tell you much about it because it isn't exactly on the market, but it recently showed up at the front door and I have been using it ever since." Ginger explained. "Thank you very much for noticing."

Wayne let out a sigh of relief and went back to pulling down sheets. The thunder rolled and the lightning struck. Both Wayne and Ginger hastily finished up getting the last of the sheets down. Wayne handed his final load to Ginger and she passed him to place them in the basket. As she passed, she turned back and noticed the rip in Wayne's pants. "Oh, dear. Looks like you've gone an tore your drawers." She plopped the sheets down into the basket on top of the carton of eggs and put both hands out beckoning Wayne over. "Let me take those and get them sewed up."

"Right here?" Wayne looked around the wide-open field.

"Are you worried about someone seeing you in your underpants?" Ginger joked. "We're the only ones around and besides you're the Master of this estate. Ain't nobody going to poke fun at you." Ginger's fingers called for his pants incessantly.

Wayne choked up the courage and dropped his pants down around his ankles and slipped his feet out of them. Before he could bend over to pick them up for Ginger, she had already snatched them and tossed them on top of the pile of sheets.

"Have these back to you quicker than the shake of a lamb's tail." Ginger took the basket and strutted off towards the house. "Have to rewash all these linens anyway."

It was a few moments before Wayne moved and another loud and awfully close thunder crash shook him from his embarrassed shock.

He entered the house via a very awkward sneak, hiding the front of his boxer briefs as he went. Wayne rapidly scanned the area for anyone who might see him in such a delicate state. Finally convinced there was no one around, Wayne relaxed and began to make his way up the stairs to his room to get a change of pants. Upon placing his empty hand on the banister, he realized he was no longer holding the carton of eggs. Patting down his body in some ridiculous attempt to find them hidden on his body he also discovered the lack of a certain letter he was tasked to deliver. Both items must currently be on their way back to the laundry room to be washed with the rest after the storm.

"Oh, crap."

Chapter 14

The sloppy slap of a palm against a doorknob popped through the hall. Wayne forced himself into a bedroom along the hall. Inside were countless American Girl dolls all still inside their respective boxes except one that was placed in the center of the room. Wayne rapidly pressed the call button for Ginger. A few moments passed and Wayne bobbed his head in and out of the room to check if she was coming. After a couple minutes Wayne understood that Ginger was clearly not as on top of things as Morese was, so he proceeded to press the button for Morese. Seconds after touching the tip of the button Morese appeared in the doorway just as Wayne bobbed his head out into the hall. This sudden appearance set off another one of Wayne's famous stumbles. Falling backwards, Wayne was stopped by a single armed grasp from Morese just before landing on a stack of American Girl Dolls dating back to 1989.

"How may I be of service, Sir?" Morese addressed Wayne while still holding him inches above the dolls.

"I need to find Ginger. She was going to do laundry!" Wayne gasped out while trying to balance himself without the help of Morese.

"Very well. The machines are quite loud in the laundry room. There is a chance she did not hear your call. Allow me to show you the way." Morese pulled Wayne to an upright position with only one arm. Wayne caught his footing and looked Morese's elderly body over trying to find where that strength came from. This only further solidified Wayne's self-pity about his own physical prowess.

Morese immediately headed off down the hall without a second thought. Wayne quickly followed.

"Hey thanks! Actually, I'm trying to retrieve something she took, well, something I left in my pocket. That she then took. Along with my pants. Because they were ripped. She didn't just take my pants. By the way that's why I'm not wearing pants. Because they ripped. And she took them."

"Here we are, Master Wayne." Morese pointed to a door with a brass sign engraved with the word Laundry.

"That makes a lot of sense." Wayne tapped one finger to his lips while subsequently pointing the sign. "But you have to admit, in this place, things aren't typically that obvious."

"This time it appears they are." Morese nodded.

"Hold on a second." Wayne entered the laundry room. The machines inside roared. Motors turned and laundry tumbled. The room was hot as Wayne passed a tube that spat lent down a chute leading straight down. There was about a three-inch gap from where the lent exited and the chute took over. Wayne stuck his head close and looked down but saw nothing except for clumps of lent blowing past and the steady almost calming hum of the dryers. He pulled away and heard what he only could compare to a hungry stomach finally receiving food. Shrugging it off at this point was the best course of action until it was an issue. Pipes casted steam and through the mist he could see Ginger tossing the sheets into the wash. Upon seeing this image Wayne rushed through the steam not realizing how hot it fell to the ground holding his face. The steam stopped and Ginger rushed over and pulled him out.

"Oh dear! I would have brought your pants to you when they were done." Ginger propped Wayne up against the washer. She blotted a sheet against his face. "You should have just waited for the steam cycle to stop. It's about ten seconds on and ten seconds off."

Wayne gave her as much of a sarcastic stare as he could. "I need my pants."

"Like I said, I'm not a speedster. I will bring them to you when I'm done with them."

"No, just for a moment." Wayne blinked his eyes tight and wide until finally being able to keep them open. "There's something in them."

"Oh! Of course." Ginger brought Wayne's pants over and gave them to him.

Wayne wasted no time and went straight to the pocket he had put the letter O'Connor gave him in. "Got it!" He handed the ripped trousers back to Ginger.

"You didn't have to go through such a fuss over that." Ginger assured Wayne. "I always go through all the pockets before washing anything. Even if they don't have pockets." Ginger giggled.

Wayne focused through the haze of the room and for a moment could have sworn Ginger looked his age.

"Is there anything else I can get you?"

"Eggs."

"Eggs?"

"I think I left some in your basket."

"Master Wayne." Ginger blushed. "I'm flattered, but I think you have it backwards."

"No!" Wayne said abruptly. "I left a carton of chicken eggs in your laundry basket."

"Oh!" Ginger's blush grew more red. "Of course. One second." Ginger stood and dug through the basket of sheets and found the carton of eggs and returned to Wayne. "These?"

Wayne took the eggs and rubbed his eyes clean of the last of the pain. "Thank you, Ginger." He turned and started to leave, but the pipes let out a burst of steam. Given he had ten seconds, he chose to use them to compliment Ginger yet again. "I'm clearly not good at complimenting women, but that new product plus this steam is really working for you." The steam stopped and he rushed through just in time.

"Thank you." Ginger said while the steam shot out and concealed her face.

In the hall Morese checked his pocket watch as Wayne appeared through the doorway. Morese immediately stood at attention.

"Got it!" Wayne held up the letter.

"Eggs?" Morese raises an eyebrow.

"Don't worry about it. The letter, O'Connor told me to give it to you." Wayne explained as he handed the letter to Morese and then using his finally free hand he rubbed the slight burn on his face. "He found it on Mrs. Fairweather's grave."

Morese reached into his pocket and pulled out a knife with a handle inlaid with gold leaf and cut open the letter. Holding the envelope in one hand he read the letter to himself. Wayne could see through the paper and noticed it was quite a long letter, but he couldn't make out any of the words. Reading backwards through paper wasn't on his list of mastered skills.

"Oh dear." Morese's face became even more pale than his fragile skin already could stand.

"What is it?" Wayne took a step forward to see what the letter said, but Morese ran off down the hall. His speed astonished Wayne, but at the same time explained his ability to respond to a call so quickly. "I really hope Mrs. Fairweather isn't writing letters from the grave now. Phone calls are one thing. Letters? That's got to take a lot of ghost energy. Let alone require the use of a ghost post office. Ghost post. Nice." Wayne looked around the hall. "And I'm talking to myself."

Wayne poked his head around the doorway to the kitchen and saw Santiago. Santiago had his back to Wayne. He was in a frantic state grabbing objects from the table and putting them into something that was right in front of him. Wayne couldn't see what exactly it was. His mind instantly went to more delicious food. Trials of Errands really builds an appetite.

"I got em!" Wayne popped in holding the carton of eggs out in front of him like a child presenting his latest macaroni masterpiece to a parent.

Santiago turned and slammed a duffel bag down on the counter. He wasn't wearing his usual chef's shirt and apron, instead he was wearing a ribbed turtleneck and canvas pants adorned with several pockets.

"What's with the cargo pants?" Wayne asked.

"They're tactical trousers." Santiago explained in a short and stern tone.

"Oh. Well I got your 'coo coo berries.'"

"No time for that."

Wayne paused for a moment with arms still outstretched and soon slumped into a very improper posture. "I'm sorry. What about the Trail of Errands?"

"Something more pressing has come up."

"Explain."

"The note you delivered from Mrs. Fairweather's grave to Morese…"

"Which I assumed was a part of the Trial."

"…was from Josie."

"Why did Josie leave a letter on Mrs. Fairweather's grave for O'Connor to give to me to give to Morese? She could have just given it to him herself." Wayne set the eggs down and walked closer to Santiago.

"The letter wasn't for O'Connor to give to you to give to Morsese, it was to Mrs. Fairweather telling her she was leaving to find the secret of the Burning Forest."

"Theeeee….burning what?" Wayne asked timidly.

"Forest. On this estate exists a forest that is in a perpetual state of flame. No one has dared venture into it because in doing so, one would surely die!" Santiago slammed first aid gear into his duffle bag.

Morese entered decked out in full trekking gear that Wayne recognized from old Egyptian expedition documentaries he'd watch in history class. "Is everything ready?" Morese asked Santiago.

"Si, we're ready." Santiago zipped up the bag. "Just need to get Senór Morris fitted up."

"Sorry, what?"

Morese turned to Wayne. "Miss Josie is in great danger. We must go and find her before it is too late." The seriousness of Morese's face burned Wayne more than the steam from the laundry room. Wayne was speechless as Santiago slung his duffel bag over his shoulder and Morese adjusted his expeditioners helmet.

"Burning forest? Nah, I'm good."

Chapter 15

The carton of eggs sat alone and neglected on the counter in Santiago's kitchen while Wayne, Morese and Santiago discussed their plan. Twelve shelled and unfertilized yokes resting and waiting for their moment to nourish. Each egg was a story waiting to be cracked. Each had a purpose. Some would be scrambled or over easy while some would be mixed with flour and make a cake. The possibilities of this single carton of eggs was endless, that is until all twelve eggs were used.

"I'm not sure I'm comfortable with this plan." Wayne struggled out.

"Josie will surely die if we do not make an effort to save her." Santiago pulled out a knife, this time it was a hunting knife that doesn't really belong in the kitchen.

"You guys weren't there. I froze when she was attacked by that swamp octopus."

"I do apologize, Sir, but an octopus has eight tentacles. The remains that O'Connor brought back to study indicated this beast had at least twelve." Morese bowed as he corrected Wayne.

"Then a whatever twelve is 'pus!' Regardless, I don't think I am a fit companion on a journey like this." Wayne walked over to the fridge. He opened the door to heaven in search of some comfort food.

"Close the fridge." Santiago commanded.

"Last time I checked; I just became the owner of all of this!" Wayne grabbed a block of Havarti and stepped away from the fridge leaving the door wide open.

"I do apologize again, Sir, but you have yet to sign the ownership papers so technically the estate still remains in a state of flux." Morese explained very cautiously.

Wayne had just taken a large bite from the block of cheese. He looked at Morese, then over to Santiago. After a moment of awkward staring, Wayne inched his way over and using his shoulder shut the fridge door. "I'm keeping the cheese."

"Do you see that carton of eggs?" Santiago pointed to the carton on the counter.

"You mean the ones you asked me to get for you, but didn't even bother to say thank you or acknowledge I even brought them? Those eggs?"

"I never wanted the eggs. It wasn't ever about that." Santiago walked over to a window on the back half of the kitchen. He pulled the curtains open to reveal a large grassy area full of chickens. "All of my eggs come from these lovely ladies."

Wayne slopped the block of Havarti down on the counter and walked over to the window. He gazed out on dozens of free-range chickens. "Then why did you send me to get you a carton of eggs."

Santiago was already over by the carton of eggs that Wayne brought. He popped open the lid. "Not a single egg was harmed."

"So what?"

"So, if you can take care of a carton of eggs through the trek you've been on, it means you have a protector in your heart. You have what it takes to protect Josie." Santiago shut the lid and tossed the eggs into the sink resulting in every one breaking.

Wayne lunged forward. "Why? Those were perfectly good eggs!"

"They were produced in cages and preceded by the hundreds with no care given to the chicken that laid them."

Wayne relaxed. "Fair enough." Wayne sulked over to Santiago and Morese. "I guess I just don't see how protecting a carton of eggs remotely relates to protecting a human life."

"It's a metaphor, Sir."

"Thank you, Morese."

"Time is of the essence. We must act quickly." Santiago said sternly.

"I can just call her and tell her to come back." Wayne pulls out his phone. "We just ate our SIM cards for this very sort of reason."

Wayne dialed Josie's number. He waited patiently on the surface, but there was an inner panic party happening as evidenced by the constant tapping of his foot. On the other end, the phone rang and rang and rang, but it wasn't Josie's voice that finally answered. Instead Wayne received the following message.

"You have reached the voice mailbox for 9...1...8...5...5...5...2...2...0...8 is not available. Please leave your name and number after the beep." Wayne waited a few seconds and finally the beep chimed in his ear.

"Josie! Please answer! I know I messed up, but you can't go into the forest. It's too dangerous!" Wayne yelled into his phone.

"Not going to work, Senor." Santiago explained. "The fire that covers the canopy is too dense for a cell signal to penetrate."

"But the tower said that we could connect to anyone in the universe. Is this forest not in the universe?" Wayne argued with intense desperation.

"Surely you didn't expect everything to be as easy as eating a SIM card." Santiago calmly retorted. "There are limitations to the power of the tower. However, perhaps you're right and the signal did reach her phone, but she is not in possession of it."

"Why wouldn't she have her phone? The cell phone was intended to be a phone you always have on you. If that weren't the case, people would still have house phones."

"You have a house phone, Sir." Morese pointed to the landline phone in the kitchen that Wayne had used not long ago to call Josie in the first place.

"Well this house is super old!" Wayne justified his remark with great defense.

"If you three are all done arguing the finer points of telecommunication, I believe I should inform you lot that what you're planning on doing is a suicide mission." O'Connor entered the kitchen and grabbed a raw carrot from a box of produce and bit into it. The crack echoed through the silence of the kitchen.

"Do you have a better plan?" Santiago asked.

"What is your plan? March off into the burning woods; a one-legged man, another on the verge of death, and a boy who pisses his pants at the sight of danger? Then what? Burn to death yourselves?" O'Connor took another hefty bite of carrot.

"We could put out the fire." Wayne offered the very logical solution of fighting fire with water.

"Good idea." O'Connor tapped the half-eaten carrot against his head in what appeared to be deep thought. "However, there is one problem. Even though it often takes scores of men and women armed with high powered water hoses and aerial technology to fight massive wildfires around the world, say you do end up dousing the flames of a few trees. You want to know what happens then?"

"What?" Wayne asked knowing he was going to be made a fool of.

"Those trees act like trick birthday candles your mean old dad put on your fifth birthday cake to be funny. Shortly after you blow one out it lights itself back up." O'Connor finished his carrot.

Wayne, Santiago, and Morese stood in silence.

"My dad did put trick candles on my birthday cake, but I was six, not five. And if I correctly remember the only way, we put them out eventually was by pulling them from the cake and dunking them in water." Wayne began to pace the room.

"You plan to pluck the trees from the ground and dip them in a cup of water?"

"Okay, O'Connor. Stop being a dick and follow me." Wayne pushed past O'Connor and out of the kitchen. The rest followed with O'Connor brought up the tail.

Wayne rushed up the stairs and into his bedroom. He walked over to the ornate chair he stood on to touch the sword and presented it to the three men with both hands. "Ta da!"

"It's a chair." Santiago said dully.

"I knew you had nothing. You need to accept that she is most likely gone forever." O'Connor explained.

Wayne felt discouraged. Surely, they knew what this chair could do. He hung his head and felt fear and sadness overwhelm him. Did he dream that the chair filled the room with water?

"Sir." Morese spoke up. "Sit in the chair, will you?"

Wayne's head shot up. Morese gave him a slight smile and nod and Wayne, moving faster than he'd ever moved before and just before he sat, he turned to the men, "Hold your breath." He sat down and the room instantly filled with water. Santiago, O'Connor, and Morese floated up off the ground and before they floated too high Wayne got out of the chair returning the room to normal. The three men fell to the floor.

"Dios mio."

"The bloody hell?"

"Mrs. Fairweather won that chair in a bet with a man in Greece over whether she could swim to the Island of Crete and back by herself. She did and he rewarded her with this chair. One of the last relics from the lost city of Atlantis." Morese explained.

"Why isn't anything wet?" O'Connor asked while feeling the rug.

"How are we all so dry?" Santiago felt his clothes and stared at Morese confused.

"That is mystery we do not know." Morese explained. "Perhaps it's an illusion or maybe another dimension. I'm sure we'll find out one day, but for now I think we've found our solution."

"Should we test this first?" O'Connor asked. "Perhaps, maybe we light a match? I'm not hauling some magic chair out there for nothing."

"There is no time." Santiago said assertively.

"Yes, there is. It's Josie. Do it, O'Connor." Wayne asserted. O'Connor pulled an old tattered and worn matchbox from his pocket. The cover had a pin-up model on it with the brand name "Mean Lady Matches." He pulled one match out and struck it along the well travelled strike zone of the box. The flame sparked forth and Wayne took his cue. The rest braced themselves this time expect O'Connor. Wayne sat, the room filled with water, Wayne stood, the match was extinguished and smoking in the hand of O'Connor was rising from the floor again.

Wayne let out a short and happy laugh and walked over to help O'Connor up. "So, you coming with us?"

Chapter 16

The heat from the flames could be felt fifteen acres away from the edge of the forest. There was no smoke coming from the tops of the trees, just clean burning fire. O'Connor's truck rattled and shook as they drove through the field leading up to the forest. Morese and Santiago rode in the cab with O'Connor while Wayne was stuck riding in the bed holding onto the Atlantis Chair. As they got closer Wayne stood up and held onto the roof of the cab and stared in wonder at the vast forest fire before him.

O'Connor slammed on the breaks and Wayne's chest bashed into the roof of the cab causing him to fall back into the bed. The three other men got out of the truck and looked in at Wayne writhing around holding his chest.

"The hell is wrong with you, boyo?" O'Connor asked while he circled around the back of the truck and popped down the tailgate.

Wayne caught his breath and crawled out of the truck. "Nothing. Just making sure my ribs still work."

"So, we place the chair near the forest and Senor Wayne takes a seat. Then poof, no more fire?" Santiago reviewed the plan.

"Essentially." Wayne nodded. "But only for a moment. So, I guess I gotta be fast."

"Let's get to work then." O'Connor took hold of one side of the chair and Wayne the other. The two men walked the chair over to about fifty feet outside the edge of the forest battling waves of heat blasting at them.

"This is a nice change. I usually have to drag chairs around by myself." Wayne joked, but O'Connor clearly didn't understand.

They placed the chair and Wayne took a deep breath and sat down. The area filled with water and the men, now armed with weights to keep them grounded looked toward the forest. What they witnessed caused them all to almost lose their breath. Wayne hopped up out the chair and the flames returned.

"Did you see that?" Wayne asked the others.

"Si. It appears the water only covers a small circumference and will not be effective against the entire forest."

"That and the damn flames came back. Bloody hell!"

"What if we put the chair back in the bed of the truck and drive it in while I sit?" Wayne suggested.

"The truck can't float!" O'Connor protested.

"Okay. I'm sure there's a submarine on this land somewhere. Or in a lake, I mean."

"Si, there is, but it is much too far away. We have no time."

"Okay, I won't sit and we'll drive in really fast."

"Tires would melt in seconds." O'Connor kicked the rubber.

"These are all marvelous ideas, Sir, but I'm terribly afraid there is one thing we haven't accounted for."

"What?" Wayne got extremely close to Morese.

"That would be," Morese took a couple steps back, "the number of people going into the forest and the number we hope to return." Morese explained.

"What do you mean?" Wayne pulled at his shirt to relieve the heat coming off the forest and getting trapped in his clothing.

"We only have the two oxygen tanks. That means only one person can enter the forest. Had the Atlantis Chair covered the entire forest one person could swim in and bring her out safely, given she can hold her breath long enough for you to get there. If we have someone driving that adds a person to the total number of tanks we'd need."

"So, what do we do? Go buy another tank?" Wayne tried to resolve the matter.

"There's no time. You'll need to go in alone. Use one of the scuba tanks to breath like a fireman and drag the chair behind you to use whenever the flames get too hot. Sitting in the chair briefly will keep you from burning alive in there." O'Connor explained.

"If I can burn alive so easily then how do we even know she's still alive?" Wayne asked.

"We don't, Senór. But we have to hope she is."

"Great. Looks like I'm dragging this chair anyway."

Santiago rigged up a harness using ropes and nylon tie down straps while O'Connor fitted Wayne with the scuba tank.

"This is your mouthpiece. You will breathe using it." O'Connor went over the basic points of the scuba gear. "When you fill your world with water you may have some water enter the regulator. If this occurs use this nozzle to purge the water from the hose. If you don't, you will drown."

"Perfect." Wayne nodded.

Santiago attached his surprisingly well made homestyle harness to Wayne and O'Connor placed the second tank in the chair carefully. Nothing happened. "Well, I guess it only works when a human sit in it." O'Connor surmised.

"You are all ready to go, Senor." Santiago placed his hand on Wayne's shoulder. "Remember, you can do this. You took care of the eggs after all." Santiago walked away and O'Connor approached.

"Don't fail her again." O'Connor didn't even so much as shake Wayne's hand and walked away.

Morese made his way over to Wayne and looked him square in the eye. "That girl is far too important to be lost now. You must bring her back at all costs."

Wayne wasn't sure what Morese meant but promised him he would. Facing the burning forest, Wayne took a deep breath and began walking in, dragging the chair behind him.

Chapter 17

Wayne had always enjoyed a nice hour in the sauna, or a cold beer in the old 1980's era hot tub at his apartment community center, but the heat coming off of the burning canopy of the forest was on the level of ten Thanksgiving dinners being prepared in the same kitchen at the same time. If not much worse. Probably worse.

The fire itself remained toward the tops of the trees which turned the area between the canopy and the ground into a natural occurring oven. If you can consider a forest that is perpetually engulfed in flames, natural. Dragging the chair was easier this time with the help of the harness and the addition of a couple old water skis Santiago fashioned to the legs, but the physical requirement it took to pull was still beyond what Wayne was normally capable of doing.

Sweat poured down his face and it wasn't long into the trek that Wayne had to take a moment and sit and rest. He sat in the Atlantis chair to cool off. He sat, water flooded around, and at first, he felt a weird panic of being able to breath in and out of water perfectly. He noticed the field of water had its limits of about twenty-five yards around.

The clock was ticking, and Wayne knew he couldn't rest for long. Just as he was getting up, he noticed something floating just at the edge of the water line. He stood and watched the object drop to the ground. Running as fast as he could with the chair weighing him down, he made his way over to the object. It was Josie's cell phone.

The purple case with a unicorn sticker on the back was undeniable. He picked it up and saw the missed call and voicemail he had left her. They were both marked as unread. Wayne realized that wherever in the forest Josie was, she had no idea he was coming for her. There must be some clue to where she went from that point. No way did Josie drop her phone on purpose. Either it fell from her pocket or she dropped it in a struggle. Thinking back to his video game experience, Wayne began to look around for signs of a struggle. He wished it was as easy as pressing a key on the controller to pop into a hyper senses mode that would allow him to view only what could possibly be clues to her whereabouts, but this was real life and no such function existed. At least none that he knew to be available to him in that moment. He'd probably gain that skill on his phone in some other new adventure where he has to plug his phone charger into his own nose to unlock it. This was all so much to get a grip on. And of course, he was standing in a constant forest fire having recently ate his SIM card to gain universal cell coverage and holding the only person's phone he'd likely be calling. Does that affect my data plan? Wayne's mind wandered. He shook off his brief A.D.D. moment and searched the ground for footprints.

Everything on the forest floor looked the same. Leaves and dirt and more leaves and dirt. The only tracking knowledge Wayne possessed was what he learned from TV and movies. Were there any broken limbs or sticks nearby? Did someone or something poop behind a bush? Would checking the area with a blacklight help in this situation? It seemed to always be the case in pretty much every crime drama. Despite knowing he didn't possess special powers; Wayne placed his fingers to his temples anyway just to see if it helped him focus. He'd seen that on TV as well.

Leaves and dirt, leaves and dirt, leaves and lines in the dirt, leaves and dirt, and wait. Lines in the dirt? Wayne got down close to the lines and could see leaves were kicked around them. Surely these marks were made by Josie. Someone or something took her. Wayne jolted up in a panic and looked all around. He couldn't see anything or anyone. Adrenaline took over and he no longer was concerned about the heat. The lines continued deeper into the forest, so Wayne took off in their direction with the chair in tow.

The spare air tank clanged and bounced in the Atlantis Chair as Wayne darted through the trees. Up ahead he could see a clearing. There didn't appear to be any flames, and this was probably since there were no trees. Josie had to be there. Wayne rushed as fast as he could to the clearing.

As he got closer, he noticed trees were cut down and laying on their side resulting in the first ground level flames he had seen so far. They were placed in a perimeter around the clearing as some sort of defense. Wayne slowed down. He felt eyes peering at him from somewhere but wasn't quite sure where. Whoever cut down those trees and built this makeshift wall did it for a reason and that reason was likely to keep people like himself and Josie out. Wayne kneeled in his best sneaking crouch, one that he modeled off several video games he mastered that required stealth movement to accomplish tasks. Unfortunately, Wayne didn't have the leg strength or flexibility to maintain such a position and after about five or so steps he stood up quickly and went about kicking his legs to the side to work out the cramps.

Focused on his incredibly out of shape legs and dancing around like an idiot in a burning forest with a chair tethered to his back, Wayne failed to notice the ten-foot-tall bear standing just a few feet away. The bear was covered in flames that whisked off his fur like he was covered in the fire equivalent of Rain-ex, but it remained around him fluttering and bending with every movement. The Fire Bear stood tall and raised its paws, baring its teeth and mighty claws. Wayne was bent over rubbing his thighs and making strange whoosh noises through his oxygen tank hose. The Fire Bear snarled and inched closer, Wayne none the wiser. Standing awkwardly in anger behind the man who clearly wasn't paying attention, the Fire Bear let its guard down and waited for Wayne to finish his odd pain relief exercise. Nearly a whole minute passed, and Wayne finally stood up, adjusted the oxygen tank and looked back to check on the Atlantis Chair. Upon turning back around to head closer to the clearing he noticed the smoking, charred rear feet of the Fire Bear standing in front of him, tapping impatiently into the dirt. Wayne's gaze tracked up Fire Bear's body, which was covered in scars. His eyes first met the bear's large and strong looking snout, but he didn't stop there. Wayne kept looking up until he finally met with Fire Bear's gleaming red eyes that were fixed up and off into the canopy with a rather annoyed look about them. Realizing the bear wasn't looking, Wayne attempted to turn and sneak off the other direction, but upon trying out his sneaking pose again his legs cramped up and he let out a loud and agonizing groan. Fire Bear's eyes snapped back to Wayne and Wayne's eyes snapped back to Fire Bear. Wayne, seeing the bear covered in fire, ran toward the Atlantis Chair, but right before he reached the cushion Fire Bear snatched up Wayne's right leg and held him upside down. The harness that attached Wayne to the Atlantis Chair snapped from the sudden jolt and weight of the chair itself.

Dangling inches from Fire Bear's face, Wayne calmly reached up and removed the oxygen mask and smiled.

"Excuse me," Wayne glanced down between the bear's legs, but all he could see was fur, "Sir?" Wayne looked back up to the bears fiery shoulders, "Did you know that you're on fire?"

Fire Bear opened his great big jaw and let out a monstrously loud roar. Drool and snot flew out and hit Wayne in the face. The bear's breath smelled exactly like gasoline and caused Wayne to nearly throw up. He quickly put his mask back on for fresh air. Fire Bear marched into his circle of cut down flaming trees with Wayne still dangling. Wayne looked around and saw a cage made of thick branches and inside, huddled in a corner, was Josie.

Wayne reached to take off his mask again to call to her, but Fire Bear dropped him, and Wayne crashed to the ground nearly breaking his neck. The oxygen tank was heavy on his back, but the weight was soon lifted when the bear ripped it away and tossed it near the perimeter of the clearing. Wayne was able to breath well in the clearing until the wind was knocked out of him with a hard slam against a tree stump. Fire Bear went to work tying Wayne to the stump and when he was done, he stomped off and out of the clearing.

Wayne waited a moment and when he was certain the bear wouldn't be returning right away, he yelled in a whisper to Josie. "Psst! Josie." Josie was drained and weary but managed to open her eyes and see Wayne. "I'm here to rescue you." Wayne said with a confident smile.

"You're not doing a very good job." Josie said after a moment checking out Wayne's current situation.

"I brought the chair."

"Oh, good. The floor was getting pretty uncomfortable."

"It's a special chair."

"For me? You shouldn't have."

"Listen, I know you're upset with me, but everything is going to be okay. Trust me."

"You shouldn't have come here, Wayne." Josie turned away. "Now, we're both going to die."

Wayne, realized she had zero faith in him and hung his head. She was right. He wouldn't be able to get them out of the Burning Forest.

Chapter 18

Wayne struggled with his restraints. How could he possibly save Josie while tied to a stump? Outside the burning tree barrier that surrounded the clearing Wayne could hear Fire Bear returning. Thumping into the ring of fire, Fire Bear had a line with several fish attached that were being cooked by the flames on his shoulders. In the other hand was the Atlantis Chair. The bear tossed the chair aside with ease and the spare oxygen tank rolled out and the mouthpiece flopped down near Wayne's hands.

Fire Bear pulled each fish off the line one by one and tossed them onto a long slab of stone over a fire that sat in the center of the clearing.

Wayne looked down at the mouthpiece. He could almost reach it if he could just get a little more slack on the rope.

"Why are you here?" Fire Bear bellowed in perfect English as he slapped another fish on the slab.

Wayne instantly forgot about the mouthpiece and reacted rather stupidly to the sight of a talking bear. "You talk?"

"I'm a bear with undying flames on my shoulders living in a forest fire and you're surprised that I talk?" Fire Bear slapped the last fish hard on the slab.

Wayne sat stunned and remembered his plan. In order to buy some time, he decided to keep the bear talking. "So, where did you get the fish?"

"Now that's a better question." The bear sat down on a stump and watched the fish sizzle. "There's a stream not far from here. I should take you sometime."

"Really?" Wayne was taken off guard at how genuine the offer sounded.

"No, I'm going to kill you and your little girlfriend." The bear flipped a few of the fish over.

"She's not my girlfriend, but that's beside the point." Wayne's fingers inched closer and closer to the mouthpiece. "Why do you need to kill us? You seem to have a nice place here. Just let us go and we won't bother you again."

"I need to send a message."

"Well! I have a phone in my pocket! Just come untie me and I can show you how to send a message. As a matter of fact, my phone can send a message to anyone in the universe. Just ask Josie." Wayne pointed with his head to Josie.

Fire Bear looked over at the weary Josie.

While the bear's head was turned, Wayne made a long thrust and managed to grab the mouthpiece and tuck it behind him. "Right, Josie? We ate plastic."

"Would you shut up?" Fire Bear bellowed.

"Yes, Wayne. You're making him angry." Josie spoke up.

"I'm sorry. I was just trying to help." Wayne smiled at Josie and gave her a wink. Josie squinted back not sure what he meant.

"Thank you. That is very kind of you. I may take you up on that offer. Send a picture of your battered bodies to everyone in the universe so they know never to enter my forest again!" As Fire Bear grew more and more angry the flames on his shoulders grew and turned blue.

Wayne had managed to take apart the mouthpiece and found a small sliver of metal that connected the hoses to it. He proceeded to rub the metal on the rope to cut himself free, meanwhile glancing and judging the distance between himself and the Atlantis Chair, which was presently on its side. "Why would a bear want to live in a forest fire anyway? Based on everything I know; bears don't really take kindly to forest fires."

"You're right." Fire Bear stared at Wayne. Wayne stopped his sawing instantly. "Fire killed my family. A human entered the forest and made camp. The next day he poured some water on the remaining embers and felt he'd done a good enough job. He left the forest after his little camping trip and shortly after a leaf fell onto his still smoldering fire. The leaf caught fire and the wind blew. The burning leaf lit more leaves on fire setting off a chain reaction that scorched everything around. I was down by the river getting fish for my family when I heard their screams." Fire Bear grabbed a fish and bit its head off. "When I found them, they were already dead. In that moment I called to the heavens and begged for a curse for this forest to burn for all time and that no living being survives here except me and those I deem worthy."

"Harsh." Wayne was terrified but tried to remain composed. "Why would you want to live where your family died?"

"The ashes that make up this dirt is all I have left of them. And as long as this central fire, started by a careless human, burns it will remain mine."

"You got the whole villain telling all the secrets of how to beat you thing down." Wayne laughed. Josie shot eyes at him. She crawled over to the edge of the cage and grabbed hold of the limbs and shook her head at Wayne.

"Beat me?" Fire Bear laughed. Wayne laughed back and Fire Bear laughed again. "Tied to a stump and trapped in a cage? I am a bear with fire in my heart and fire on my body. I will make an example of you, you cocky human."

"Don't hold your breath." Wayne smiled. "I mean she might want to hold hers, but you? I wouldn't recommend it."

"What the hell are you talking about?"

"It's a saying. Don't hold your breath. Like, don't wait for that to happen. You'll die." Wayne winked at Josie. "So, you, Mr. Fire Bear. Is it Mister? Doesn't matter. Don't hold your breath." Wayne paused. "Josie." Wayne nodded.

"I told you to shut up!" Fire Bear stood up and threw a fish at Wayne. Wayne dodged the fish and with one final pull of his makeshift saw, he severed his restraints and lunged for the Atlantis Chair.

"Josie! Hold your breath!" Wayne rolled into the Atlantis Chair sideways and the clearing flooded with water. Josie, at the last minute, held her breath and then floated to the top of the cage, pressed tight against the limbs. Wayne held tight to the chair and watched the fire under the slab go out. The cooked fish floated up and seemed to swim around the now extinguished Fire Bear. Everything was floating. Fire Bear pawed wildly to stay still. Wayne noticed the cage Josie was in started to float as well. He held tight and hoped Josie was strong enough to hold her breath until he could free her. Floating around him were the broken pieces of both oxygen tanks. Josie's body went limp and Wayne let go of the chair and pushed away. The water vanished and he fell to the ground narrowly missing the stump he had been tied to. Fire Bear wasn't as lucky and smashed hard down onto his stump chair and the cooking slab. Josie's cage crashed to the ground and shattered.

Wayne scrambled over to Josie lying in a pile of broken sticks. He shook her to try and wake her up. He glanced over at Fire Bear who now looked a lot more like just a normal bear without his flames. Wayne noticed he'd put out the central fire and the forest wasn't burning anymore. Shifting his focus back to Josie, Wayne noticed she wasn't breathing.

"Crap. My Red Cross CPR certification expired last month. I'm no longer qualified to do this." Wayne panicked for a moment and looked at her lifeless face. "Whatever, she can sue me." He laced his palms and began compressions. One, two, three, all the way to fifteen. "Geeze, that really seems like a lot." Wayne checked to make sure the bear was not moving anymore then leaned in and placed his mouth on hers. Just as his lips touched hers, Josie spit water all over Wayne's face. Josie opened her eyes and without hesitating she spoke.

"Sorry, Mr. Morris. These lips belong to O'Connor." She smiled.

"That's really, actually, disgusting." Wayne smiled back and started to help her up when the bear let out a loud roar. Wayne and Josie fell back and watched the bear writhe in pain, but not get up. "I think we should run now." Wayne helped Josie up and they ran out of the former ring of fire. Upon their exit, O'Connor, Santiago and Morese pulled up in O'Connor's truck.

"Guys! Perfect timing!" Wayne yelled.

"We saw the forest lose its flames and figured you must have done something right for once." O'Connor quipped as he hopped out with Santiago to retrieve the Atlantis Chair.

Morese wrapped a blanket around Josie and helped her into the cab. O'Connor and Santiago loaded up the Atlantis Chair and Wayne hopped in the bed with it. O'Connor fired up the engine and Santiago joined Wayne. As Wayne helped Santiago up, Fire Bear rolled over and pointed at them with his soaking wet and steaming paws.

"You ruined everything! You took my home. You took my family. I will burn yours to the ground. You just wait." The bear flopped to the ground unconscious.

"Is he dead?" Wayne asked.

"You better hope so. I left my rifle back at the house." O'Connor said as he peeled off back toward home. The truck jarred and rattled through the smoldering forest.

"Don't you worry, Senór," Santiago placed his hand on Wayne's shoulder, "that bear's back was broken. I could see it from a mile away."

"Thanks, Santiago. That's reassuring."

"And, hey. You saved the girl." Santiago pointed into the cab at Josie who was looking back at Wayne. "Which was more difficult? This or the carton of eggs?"

Wayne smiled from ear to ear at Josie and then looked at Santiago cold. "This. This was by far much harder."

Chapter 19

Still was the room before the storm of an exhausted and hard worked man came crashing in. The rug was clean, and the bed was made. Chairs and trinkets in place and the curtains were freshly ironed. Unfortunately, all that hard work put in was only done so that the master of the estate could unconsciously jump, fly, and land hard on the mattress sending pillows soaring into windows, shelves, and random important historical statues that the staff had yet to understand doesn't belong in the room of a man in his twenties who never really grew up.

"That was insane!" Wayne wiggled on the bed like a teenage girl who just barely touched the hand of her superstar crush on a red carpet for a children's version of an awards show. "Why was I such a coward before?" He popped up and stared right at Josie who stood dead center in his room twisting side-to-side holding her dress. "What?" Wayne was getting nervous.

"We kissed." Josie blushed as she dropped her head a bit just for a second.

Wayne quickly scrambled out of the bed and onto his feet. "No…no……no." He struggled to find the right words. "We…I…saved your life…with CPR. Not a kiss."

"Your lips were on mine." Josie strummed an air guitar quickly and said, "Digi digi digi digi digi! Kiss!" as one who listened to the Artist Formerly Known as Prince and then re…known as Prince again. Rest in purple.

"Doesn't make it a kiss."

"You're strange. I like that." Josie bounced and ran to his closet. "So, what are you going to wear tonight?"

"I don't know. A button up and jeans?"

"Gross. Who are you Dawson's Creek?"

"Who?"

"James Van Der Beek. My mom loved that show." Josie flipped through all three of the shirts Wayne had in his closet. "You need help."

Wayne sat back on the bed, his feet dangling above the ground a bit making him more childlike. "I don't go to fancy things a lot. Or ever."

"They are so much fun. It doesn't even matter if you know anyone or not. You just start talking and you go on so many fun adventures through others, it's magical!" Josie slammed Wayne's closet doors shut. "We need to find you a better wardrobe." She ran over to Wayne and grabbed his hand pulling him off the bed, his feet slammed on the ground, then out the door.

Wayne immediately ran back in. "Wait a second, Josie!" The documents making the estate officially his rested on a dresser. He picked up the fountain pen that was waiting for him and flipped open the folder and signed everywhere Suit Man had made an 'X.' "I might regret this, but adrenaline is running hot in my bloodstream today!"

Josie poked her head into the room and smiled. Her eyes reflected a calm and restful ease as she stared at the signature on the page.

As they traversed the house in search of a room that would possibly house garments more suitable to the evening's event a door on the first floor caught Wayne's eye. It was ornate and beautiful. Something unlike any of the other doors in the house and if this door caught his eye that was saying something being that it was a door and doors are not typically a subject of uncontrollable attraction. This one was right by the front door. How did he not notice it before? It's as if now, it had a halo of glow about it.

Wayne pulled away from Josie and headed downstairs toward the door. His hands held back the urge to rub the unwashed greasiness of a young man's palms all over it. This door called to him and it was driving deep into his bones. He didn't want to make love to the door, but something about it made him love it.

His mind searched rapidly through a catalog of doors he had experienced in his life and only one came close, but was still miles away and the only thing cool about it was that the door handles were elephant faces and the part you pulled was the trunk. Other than that, he had never experienced a door quite like this.

The carvings were so delicate, but the lines were strong and deliberate. It reminded him of the carvings above his bed, but these were different. The symbols and shapes were unlike anything he'd seen before. Circles that intersect with squares, which doubled and intersected with jagged lines that resemble lightning bolts. The pattern repeated with variations at times that seemed to be more deliberate in their meaning. Some were signs of animals; bears, wolves, fish, eel, while some were more structural; bridges, mountains, pyramids, coliseums. They presented themselves as if they were accomplishments of a sort.

As his eyes groped the door his mind began to think about what the carvings meant and the closest thing he could attach such in sync randomness to, was a tattoo sleeve on a well accomplished man he had met in a bar while traveling through Texas. Some people get tattoos for fun, others are drunk out of their minds or hearts recently broken and regret their choice forever, but then there are the likes of Arnold.

Arnold was a soft-spoken man who kept generally to his own. Never been one known to get involved in the regular establishment wide bar fights that took place most Saturday's at the Sunray Saloon. He'd simply order another whiskey and wait until the ruckus settled down. He'd been coming to the Sunray for a few years now and always ordered the same thing, Bud Light in a glass with a side of tomato juice and a well whiskey neat. Ricky, the bartender, knew exactly when Arnold needed another without any words or hand gestures. It was an understood sort of thing. Wayne couldn't have been more than legal age when he thought it would be wise to show his fresh non-weathered face in that place.

It was a Saturday night and no fights had yet broken out not to say that that would not be alright. Wayne trotted his way to the bar and ordered a Pabst Blue Ribbon.

"Lone Star." Ricky mumbled as he barely wiped a glass clean.

"Excuse me?" Wayne leaned in bright eyed and bushy tailed to hear better.

"Lone Star." Ricky repeated himself a bit more clearly, but in a tone that implied Wayne was mentally challenged.

"Oh, yeah. I guess I am tonight. Ol' Lone Star." Wayne tipped an imaginary rim of his hat and spoke in a terrible Texan accent. "So, how about that PBR?"

The entire bar was silent. Everyone's attention was on young Wayne and his ignorant and embarrassing actions. Ricky slammed a bottle right down in front of Wayne spilling a bit of beer in the process, "Two fifty."

Wayne leaned in and looked at that label and it read Lone Star. "Excuse me, this is a Lone...oh." He looked around and most everyone had either a Budweiser product or a Lone Star beer in hand. "Thank you." He handed Ricky a five. "Keep the change."

"Not from around here are you?" Arnold's gravelly voice almost ripped a hole in Wayne's ear.

"I'm going to be honest. I'm sort of afraid to even ask if you're talking to me or not." Wayne's hand shook a bit as he sipped his Lone Star to prevent any more embarrassing words from leaking out.

"You're the only one in this place that doesn't feel at home in his own skin. I'd say it's pretty safe to say I'm talking to you."

Ricky moved away from the two almost acquainted strangers. Something about Arnold talking made him uneasy.

"No, no I am not. No."

"Brave."

"Wh...what?"

"I've seen your kind come in here before. Young, stylish sort. They're looking for a "hole-in-the-wall" to tell all their friends about." Arnold sipped his whiskey neat. "They never make it past the door."

"Why?" Wayne looked around the room to make sure he wasn't in any danger.

"They're wimps."

Wayne took a moment to figure out if he should be proud, he made it past the door or scared for the same reason. There were two men playing pool. One had an incredibly long beard, which he tossed over his shoulder to take his shot. The other stood stoic with his cue upright and centered with his body. His head was shaved and had Hatin' Like Satan tattooed along the side. Over in the corner where the cues were stored Wayne could only make out one or two other cues that were intact. The rest were split and splintered or outright broken in half forming perfect makeshift spears if the mood struck. Across the rest of the bar were tables filled with other men slamming shots and smoking cigarettes. Other tables were sites of the ancient mating rituals of road warriors whose faces were as leathered as the vests on their backs. Equally haggard and experienced women sat on their laps drinking Lone Star and running their free hand over the slightly toned upper arms of these nefarious men. One man sat alone with an entire bottle of bourbon and a single shot glass just sharpening his knife. Fast asleep at his feet laid a dog that didn't seem to mind the noise. Thing about this dog that was odd was that it was in fact a Pomeranian, which only made the man with the knife seem that much scarier. Wayne turned back to the bar and took a long pull off his beer.

"Trust me, boy. You're not a wimp. You're not brave either. You're just oblivious." Arnold spoke without looking at Wayne.

"Should I leave?"

"You're already here, aren't you?" Again, without a single word or gesture Ricky poured Arnold another drink and slid him a beer. This time he set Wayne up with the same. "Cheers!" Arnold raised his whiskey to Wayne who fumbled a moment before grabbing his shot.

"Cheers." Wayne held his glass out to click it against Arnold's, but Arnold simply shot his back and set the glass on the bar. With awkward hesitation, Wayne did the same and slammed his glass down. Silence once again shivered through the Sunray.

"Never slam your glass unless you're looking to start a fight." Inaudible sound trickled back.

Trying to check behind him to see if anyone had a barstool raised and ready to smash against his back without turning to look, Wayne strained his eyes as far to the corners of his sockets that he could. He looked right and saw nothing. He looked left and saw nothing. However, as he scanned back to center, he noticed that Arnold had a full sleeve of tattoos running up his arm.

None of the tattoos seemed to relate to each other in any direct way, but they were all done in the same style and presented in a pattern from his wrist and up into his actual shirt sleeve where Wayne could only assume they continued. From what was visible there must have been at least twenty different symbols stemming off single lines that started with a short perpendicular base like an upside down "T" with a shorter horizontal line. Another line zig zagged across the long line and ended at the same point ultimately pointing to the individual symbols.

Starting from the wrist just in line with his right thumb, the first symbol was a book which was open and displaying it's pages for the world to read. Wayne could only see a couple more including an old single propeller plane, what looked like a wolf, and a shot glass filled to the brim.

Arnold caught Wayne staring at his arm. "No, you can't touch them."

Wayne shook from his curious daze, "Why would I want to touch them?"

"Everyone always wants to touch them. Sometimes they don't even ask. If it's a woman, I sternly tell them to stop. If it's a man, well, let's just say the hand they use won't feel great for a few weeks."

"I don't have tattoos. Do they feel different?"

"Do you have skin?"

Wayne stupidly checked his body, but with a level of performance as to not just say yes. "I believe so, yes."

"They feel like skin."

"But, what about that guy's skin?" Wayne almost pointed but withdrew and instead did an awkward head nod to one of the leather-skinned bikers nearby.

"Don't be cute." Arnold didn't even look.

"Do you mind me asking what they all mean?"

"Yes, I do mind. But I also understand they are on display for the world to see so what I'll tell you is this. Each one symbolizes either an accomplishment in my life or a key event. As new things happen, as I do new things, I get new tattoos. Simple as that."

Wayne sat in silence for a moment. He turned to his beer. Picked at the label then finished off what was left. "Well, that was anticlimactic. All that build-up and slapped with an obvious and foreseeable answer. I'll have to say…"

"Be quiet and drink your beer."

Sliding Wayne's empty Lone Star aside, Ricky placed a Bud Light, somehow ordered for him. It was in a pint glass and Wayne lifted it to his lips and noticed Arnold pour a little bit of his tomato juice into his glass. Wayne's tomato juice sat in front of him just screaming of being one part of what seemed like a nasty combination. He grabbed the juice, to be polite, and poured just a little bit into the beer. A slight red tint made its way through the bubbling liquid as Wayne made a very cartoonish gulp in preparation for the taste to come.

"I'll tell you what." Arnold whipped his mouth with a bar napkin. "You go drink for drink with me. Same drinks. And I'll tell you my story. Deal?"

Wayne really wanted to know Arnold's story, but he also really was not a fan of Arnold's drink choices. "Deal." He reluctantly answered.

"Bottoms up, Sailor."

Arnold and Wayne chugged their tomato infused alcoholic beverages and this time Wayne made sure not to slam his glass.

"You still with me?"

Wayne opened his eyes and before him was the door with all its amazing symbols. "Hello? Spaceman. You in there?" He turned to Josie who had an overly concerned yet comical look on her face. "Thought I lost you to some sudden onset coma for a second." Josie joked. "Where did you go?"

"Just a memory. That's all."

"Well, welcome back to the present. Now, come on. We need to find you some proper clothes."

Josie headed back upstairs. "If I remember correctly, Mr. F had a huge closet up here."

Wayne rolled up his sleeve a bit just above his inner elbow and looked at a tattoo of a lone line with a short perpendicular base and a zigzag line leading up to a shot glass filled to the brim. He looked up at the symbols on the door and reached for the handled. It was locked.

"Come on! Let's play dress up!"

Wayne backed away and got back to his clothing adventure with Josie.

Chapter 20

The hall they headed down had so many doors it was hard for Wayne to believe that the Fairweather's lived here alone save for the handful of staff. What were all these rooms for? Josie opened door after door and each time she'd shut them and just uttered, "Nope," and moved on. She did this so quickly Wayne never had a chance to look inside. However, none of these rooms really concerned him. He wanted to go back to the one with the mesmerizing door. What was in that room? It must be something important because why else put so much effort into a door like that if you were just going to keep coats or boxes behind it.

"Josie, slow down a sec."

Josie stopped and turned around. "You okay?"

"Yeah. Hey, you know a lot about this house, well clearly not where a closet is, but you still know more than me. Do you know what's behind that awesome door downstairs?"

Sadness overtook Josie. Her head hung and she looked up at Wayne with eyes that could belong to a puppy that just got in trouble for peeing on the rug. "That's Mr. F's study."

"That makes so much sense!" Wayne's interest levels spiked. "Wait, why are you so sad about it?"

Josie looked up and walked over to Wayne slowly. "The thing is, that room has been locked as long as I've known. It is like the one room I've never been able to go into." Josie's demeanor shifted from sad to frustrated. "Something about Mr. F. demanding no one is to enter, punishable by exile."

"Really? Well, it's officially my house now. So, I say we go in." Wayne commanded. Josie's eyes lit up. Wayne turned around to go back to the door and was instantly met by Morese. "Yikes! You have got to stop doing that."

"Did you just audibly say, 'Yikes,' Sir?" Morese teased but remained completely stone faced.

"Did you just make a joke, Morese? Comin' out of your shell."

"I did indeed, Sir."

"What's up? Is it quick because Josie and I have a cool ass room to go into?" Wayne paused. "Sounds a lot less interesting saying it out loud like that."

"That is what I wanted to talk to you about, Sir." From behind Morese came The Suit Man walking down the hall. "No one is allowed in that room."

"Surely I am. I mean, I own this place now. It's technically my room."

The Suit Man handed Wayne the legal papers Wayne signed to take over the property. "On the contrary. Per the contract you signed it expressly states that you have complete ownership and control over all lands, assets, and structures on the estate except for that one particular room. It remains in the ownership of a trust that only Mr. Fairweather has access to."

"But he's dead." Wayne scanned the documents knowing he had absolutely no idea what he's looking for.

"Correct, but the fact still remains, you are not allowed inside. The door is locked and sealed from the inside." The Suit Man took the contract back and walked away.

"I'm very sorry, Sir." Morese turned and left them as well.

"That sucks." Wayne turned to Josie. "I'm sorry. I didn't mean to get your hopes up."

"It's okay!"

"What? A moment ago, you were all upset then mad about not being able to be inside that room. What changed?"

"We're already on an adventure. We can break into that room another time."

"What adventure?"

"Operation Fancy Dress. Duh?" Josie grabbed Wayne's arm and pulled him down the hall. She looked back at Wayne slightly flirty, "Are you feeling okay? You're like major ADHD today."

Wayne looked back down the hall behind him. "Yeah, I'm peachy."

Chapter 21

"What about this one?" Josie grabbed a dark blue suit jacket, two buttons, with a festive lining. She held it up to Wayne's chest to eyeball size.

"Yeah, sure why not."

"Take this seriously, please." Josie softly stomped her foot on the ground. It would have been more effective if it didn't come off incredibly cute.

"Any of these work as long as they fit. We just opened about thirty doors before finding this massive closet. I mean who puts their closet on the other side of their house? So ineffective." Wayne ranted while Josie ignored him and kept measuring out his size.

The closet was the size of the average American living room. There was wall to wall suits in styles spanning decades and each style neatly divided in its own section like a museum of fashion, but with a petting zoo angle where you get to try the garments on.

"Seriously, this is way too many suits for one man. I'm just going to say it. Mr. F was a hoarder."

"Maybe something with tails."

"No! Nope. Uh uh!" Wayne rushed over and grabbed Josie's hand on the hanger of a terrible tuxedo jacket. "I wore an all-white suit to prom, with tails. Took the prettiest girl in school. Fairly sure the suit was why I didn't get lucky."

"Are you expecting action tonight, Mr. Morris?" Josie gave Wayne a flirty yet judgmental eye. "Another kiss perhaps?"

"What? No. What...no!" Wayne took his hand off hers. "I'm saying no tails."

Ginger walked in holding a laundry basket and the sight of the two young fashion hunters startled her. "Oh! Goodness. You two gave me a fright. What are you doing in here?"

"Exactly!" Wayne turned to Josie. "What are we doing in here? And Ginger, why is the closet on the other side of the house from the bedroom?"

"Well, because Mr. Fairweather would usually just call Morese to bring him a suit each morning' and the staff quarters are located in this here wing."

Wayne and Josie tried to hide the sense of stupidity they felt for not thinking of that first. Josie quickly went back to flicking through suits and Wayne just stood there smiling.

"Would you two please excuse me? I have a lot of work to do in here and if I can be frank, I have this room very meticulously organized." Ginger held an uncomfortable smile on her face.

"Josie, I think we should go. For now, we can have Morese bring some options later."

"Yeah, okay. Sorry, Ginger."

Wayne and Josie shuffled out the door. Once out Ginger went over to the far side of the room and sat her basket down. Wayne popped his head back in startling her one more time.

"Sorry, can I ask you a quick question?" Wayne slid back into the room. "Why isn't anyone allowed in Mr. F's study?"

"Oh. Well, you see..." Ginger scanned for the right way to say what she wanted to. "Why don't you meet me in the library in twenty minutes. I'll tell you everything you want to know if you just let me get to my work."

"We have a library?"

"Yes. Now, please, darlin'."

"Oh, yeah, of course. I'll find it."

"Thank you." Her eyes said the rest and Wayne bowed out for good this time.

In the hall, Wayne looked around for Josie, but did not see her anywhere so he went on his own to find the library. She'll text if she's lost. Right?

Wayne patiently waited in the library that took him fifteen minutes to find. By his brilliant calculations which he was stupidly immensely proud of, he'd only have to wait five minutes for Ginger to show up on the assumption she would be on time. Wayne took this time to look around a bit. He could not remember the last time he was in a library but was sure it must have been when he was very young, and his mother would take him to participate in a summer reading club. One of those challenges that wasn't even a real challenge at all, read a book, get a stamp, get enough stamps, and get a prize. The prize was always some cheap metal with that year logo pressed on it.

There were books on these shelves he'd never even heard of before and it was likely because he'd never seen the movie version. On the other hand, he found books with titles of movies he loved and had no idea they were based on books in the first place. He picked up a copy of Jurassic Park by Michael Crichton. In doing so he told himself he would take it back to his room and read it to see if it was indeed better than the movie like everyone claims when it comes to adaptations. However, deep down he knew he'd read the introduction and stop, leaving the book to collect dust on his nightstand and maybe one day become the victim of a spill of some sort. Really, that final situation is in fact the most tragic because once a book is soaked in water, or other fluids, it is never the same. Not that Wayne necessarily had a ton of experience with moist books, but he had spilled his fair share of leftover drinks on magazines that he was really into for one reason or the other.

Something happens to paper after it encounters water. The afflicted area shrivels and pulls the surrounding paper in. The edges curl and ripple and if multiple pages meet this fate it is highly likely the book will swell to twice its original size and never close quite the same again. If you're quick enough and are willing to spend the time it is possible to save a book from this fate for the most part if a hair dryer is taken to the pages. Back and forth, back and forth, back and forth until all the pages are dry and even then, you're not guaranteed perfection.

It was about two minutes of Wayne gesturing as if he were using a hair dryer to fake dry the non-wet copy of Jurassic Park before he realized Ginger was standing nearby watching his ridiculous tutorial daydream.

"I was just pretending this book was wet and I was using a…you know what? Never mind." Wayne pantomimed placing the hair dryer down and walked over to Ginger.

"You have a good ol' imagination. That's just perfect. What I'm about to show you takes a little bit of faith and a lot a bit of imagination. Are you ready?"

"I guess so. Bring on the next unusual thing this house has to offer."

Ginger led him over to a bookshelf, which was home to countless photo albums. Each one was labeled with a month and a year and some were even labeled down to a specific event. She scanned the rows sliding her finger along the edges. The tapping and bumping noises it made built a rhythm and Wayne felt a bit transfixed. Ginger was looking better than she ever had before. Was it his 'good ol' imagination' that made him think she was an older woman when he met her? The Ginger that stood before him now couldn't be much older than he was, and it made him feel a bit uncomfortable. Everything about her was fantastic. Her face was beautiful, her arms firm and toned, her chest supple, and stomach tight. Wayne caught himself checking her out and averted his eyes. Ginger stopped on one album and as she pulled it out Wayne stole one last look at her long gorgeous legs.

"Got ya!"

Wayne shot his hand up and ran his fingers through his hair in a not so cool, cool guy casual way to try and indicate he was not doing anything inappropriate. Ginger plopped the seemingly one-ton photo album down on a nearby table. The thud echoed through the stacks and shook the floor beneath their feet.

"What were these pictures taken on, steel plates?" Wayne jested.

"No, but they were captured using a special camera designed by a strapping young chap named Nicola Tesla. Sadly, Mr. Fairweather was the only one to obtain a working prototype before Tesla's death."

"How convenient that it in no way can be linked to any historical fact. What does it do?" Wayne sarcastically remarked.

"It captures memories."

"So, it takes a picture."

"No. Beyond that." Ginger opened the photo album. At first, they appeared to be normal photos, but then Wayne noticed the perspective of the event kept changing as if it were a slideshow only subtly altering the viewpoint of the image. Parallax if you will or sort of like a GIF thumbnail.

"Are those photos moving?"

"Not quite. You see, these here photos capture the memories and perspectives of all the folks involved. Then it reconstructs them and plays back the event in real time for whoever wants to view them." Ginger explained with the sweetest and most naive tone.

"Like a movie then."

"It's better if you just see for yourself." Ginger flipped to the photo she wanted Wayne to see. It was a shot of Morese, Santiago, and O'Connor standing in front of the large wonderfully carved door. "Now, all you have to do is take your hand and touch the photo and imagine yourself there."

"What?" Wayne stepped back. "I am here. That photo was taken right downstairs. I can just walk there."

"No, not the location. The time."

"Like, time travel?" Wayne stepped a bit closer. Time travel had always been a fascination of his from the first time Doc Brown and Marty took the DeLorean back to the 1950's.

"Not exactly. You will travel to that time, but you won't be actually there. You can't change anything, and no one will see you. You simply just get to observe with those kind eyes of yours." Ginger flirted.

Wayne found himself not only with mixed feelings about Ginger, but a rush of curiosity, stepped to the photo album and reached out for the photo in question. His fingertips touched the black and white image and he closed his eyes. Moments passed and he opened them and looked around. He was still in the library with Ginger. Did it work? Am I here?

"Afraid not, dear. If you were there, you'd know it. And you most certainly wouldn't be in this room. You have to relax and believe you're there." Ginger got extremely close to Wayne and rubbed her hand up and down his back. "Think of it as a memory of your own you desperately want to revisit and live all over again."

He took a deep breath and closed his eyes. His mind was focused solely on how badly he wanted to get into that room. Again, he reached his hand out and this time, time seemed to slow down.

"Don't spend too much time in there. Every minute in a photo is exactly one minute in real life." Ginger whispered in his ear.

"So, time isn't slowing down. Heavy."

His fingers touched the photo and a tingling sensation came over his entire body. The almost pleasant pins and needles feeling only lasted a few seconds and when it was done Wayne was afraid to open his eyes. He could tell he was no longer touching anything and the room he was in didn't hold that old book smell like the library. As if it made it safer, Wayne opened one eye at a time very slowly. He could see the door right in front of him, but there was no sign of Morese, Santiago, or O'Connor. They were in the photo so why were they not right there? Wayne looked around and saw no one. The area looked very much the same as it did back in his time or rather forward in his time. Either way there wasn't much to go on to determine if he was in fact in the past or a memory of it for that matter.

The relics that adorned the hall were the same he'd seen before. Paintings hung just where he remembered. The only difference was a strange smoky odor that reminded him of roasting marshmallows at a campsite. Maybe it was the wood used to construct the house. Perhaps over time it lost its potency and by the time Wayne came around the scent was virtually gone. Wayne didn't know much about wood or the differences in their smells, but he seemed content with this assumption. That was until he turned back to the carved door and noticed actual smoke billowing out from the space underneath.

Morese came running. He was a bit younger, but still not a young man. Following him was Santiago who was quite a bit younger and had a different and cruder prosthetic.

"Dios mio! What happened?" Santiago reacted to the smoke in a much less calm and collected manner than Wayne was briefly accustomed to witnessing.

"Master Fairweather must have fallen asleep with a cigar in hand again." Morese said with a solemn calm.

Santiago rushed to the door to open it. Upon touching the doorknob his hand recoiled rapidly in pain. "Puta Madre!"

"We cannot open the door."

"Que?" Santiago got right in Morese's face. "He is going to die in there!"

"If ya open that door there you risk bringin' this whole place to the dirt." O'Connor stood in the doorway. "Now, if you'll excuse me, I'm going to take a peek in the window ta see if he's conscious. If one of you boyos wouldn't mind making sure I don't fall off the ladder and add to the possible body count that would be tip top." O'Connor walked out as calm as ever.

A short ladder was propped up against the side of the house leading up to a set of brilliantly brass-lined windows. O'Connor climbed up and stood on the very top of the ladder while Santiago and Morese held the sides for balance. Wayne stood back as a helpless bystander and watched the three men who, in his time, were tasked with making sure he was looked after do everything they could to save another.

"Oy! The smoke is dense as a London fog." O'Connor strained to see through the smoke and flame when he saw Mr. Fairweather. He was standing in the middle of the room, cigar in one hand and glass of scotch in the other. His eyes met with O'Connor and Mr. Fairweather simply raised his glass and nodded. Mr. Fairweather took a long drink and made his way to the door where he pulled a large wooden carving of a bear's head out then twisted. An extremely loud thud billowed out and was easily heard outside as Mr. Fairweather had just released several sheets of two inch thick steel plates up between the walls that connected the room to the rest of the house including over the window O'Connor was looking in. O'Connor to jumped down, grabbed his ladder and walked inside. "He's sealed the room from the inside. There's nothing we can do now."

"What?" Wayne screamed and ran after him. "You're just going to trap him in there?" The three men didn't react to Wayne's protest. Even though Wayne knew they couldn't see him, and he couldn't change what they were doing, he still tried and grabbed at their arms, but his hands just wiped through them like ghosts.

He caught up with the trio as they stood in front of the door listening to the faint sound of the room and its contents crackling in the flames. The sound of tires smashing and pushing aside the gravel driveway as Mrs. Fairweather's car pulled up and parked. The three men looked out past the invisible Wayne with dread in their hearts to tell her the bad news. Her car was rather large, and she hoped out spry as a teenager, ran around to the back and pulled an antique chair from the rear.

"Morese! O'Connor! Would one of you come help me with this? It's not that it's heavy, it's just a bit awkward to carry." Mrs. Fairweather struggled with the chair until Morese and O'Connor took over and brought it inside for her. "I won it off a Greek man. Poor sap doubted my swimming skills. He says it's from the lost city of Atlantis. Not sure I believe him, but I just really liked the cut of it. What do you think?"

Wayne's heart broke to know this fresh excitement and optimism was about to be shattered. He didn't hear Santiago break the news as the sadness of the situation was deafening. Mrs. Fairweather picked up the chair on her own and in silence carried it up to her room. The men hung their heads in silence until an unwitting Ginger rushed in with a very strange camera in hand.

"Cheese, ya'll!" She snapped a photo, the very one that brought Wayne back to this memory. "What's with the long faces? I told you to say cheese!"

Wayne wanted to leave, but the Ginger of his time never told him how. However, in that moment he was back in the library where Ginger sat reading the copy of Jurassic Park he'd previously taken down. She looked now just as she did then. It was strange, but that did noreally concern him at the moment. He excused himself and left her. She knew why and closed the book and put the photo album back on the shelf then went back to work.

Chapter 22

A barstool flew perfectly between Wayne and Arnold then smashed into a shelf full of liquor bottles shattering them all and leaving a suicide cocktail of booze and broken glass pouring down the counter. Over by the pool table a man with a broken pool cue sticking out of his thigh was beating a man's face in with the six ball and the two women previously making nice with a couple of bikers were pulling at each other's hair and both accusing the other of stealing their respective men.

Wayne had adopted Arnold's indifference to the chaos around them. The two men were four shots deep from the point of Arnold's challenge, which likely meant Arnold was really closer to seven. Ricky kept them coming and poured from a bottle he kept under the bar, safe from any flying seating.

"What possessed you to walk into a place like this?" Arnold's words expressed concern, but his tone remained stoic.

"Honestly? From the outside it looked like the most plain and boring bar I've come across so far." Wayne held his shot up for a cheer, evoking Arnold to follow suit. "Everything else in this town is themed or doubles as a record store. I just wanted a simple bar that served simple drinks. Guess I messed that up. Not the simple drinks part."

"What brings you to Texas?" Arnold continued his line of questioning.

"Hey! I'm going toe-to-toe with you here. I think I've earned the right to ask you a question for once."

For the first-time all-night Arnold turned and looked Wayne square in the eye. "You do have some balls on you under that newborn fluff. Fire away."

Wayne was bursting with excitement but held it in because he did not want Arnold to take back the balls comment. "The tattoos. What does the Roman numeral mean? That's seven, right?"

"Prison. Spent seven years for aggravated assault." Arnold stopped flat as if that was enough.

"Elaborate please." One of the bikers smashed a beer bottle on the bar between them immediately after Wayne spoke. "Because, this doesn't seem like the sort of place someone with a criminal history of assault should be in."

"I picked a fight with a fast-food mascot." Arnold blurted out quicker than he took shots. This prompted Ricky to line up another round.

"You what?" Wayne nearly spit out his tomato juice and beer combo, which he had grown to like after he was well and drunk.

"I was having a bad day. My car had been repo'd and I lost my job."

A much younger and non-tattooed Arnold sulked down the busy streets of downtown New Haven, Connecticut. Angst built up inside him and revealed itself in the form of shoulder checking incoming foot traffic as well as stepping out into oncoming vehicle traffic and slapping the hood of the cars which made sudden screeching stops in order not to kill him.

"I'm walkin' here!" Arnold screamed at the poor old lady behind the wheel of an 80's model Chevy Malibu.

"What do you think this is, New York?" The old lady hollered back accompanied by flashing her .357 Magnum. "Keep walking, you pussy!"

Arnold heeded her words and kept walking. However, nearly being shot by a little old lady didn't autocorrect his anger. His stomach began to rumble, and he remembered he'd skipped breakfast that morning because it was donut day in the employee lounge. Unfortunately, he was called into his boss's office to discuss his performance, which by the result of the conversation leaving him without a job meant it was lacking. By the time he left his firing the donuts were all gone.

A few more shoulder checks and light cursing later a flyer for a fast food chain was thrust into his chest by a grown man dressed to the nines as a clown. Arnold's first response was to hit the man, but he read the flyer offering a free cheeseburger and restrained himself. He looked at the clown and smiled for the first time that day, "Thank you." Arnold stuck the flyer in his pocket and walked on. He could have grabbed the burger right there at that location, but his apartment was about seven blocks away and he preferred to eat at home at his own table so he figured he'd hit the franchise location which was around the corner from his building.

The rest of the walk home was a little bit happier knowing he'd be able to eat that day without spending the money he was no longer in a position to regularly earn. Sure, it was just one cheeseburger, but Arnold was used to a minimalist life and could appreciate what one cheeseburger could do. Arnold walked into the restaurant chain near his building and pulled out the coupon. The cashier looked and slid it back to him. "I'm sorry, Sir. This coupon is only for participating locations and we aren't participating. Would you still like to order a cheeseburger?"

Arnold's last paycheck didn't come for another week and he'd just paid all his rent and bills for the month plus about half of each check was donated to the bar on the first floor of his apartment building in exchange for sour mash. He didn't have a penny to his name. Enraged at his string of bad luck he grabbed the flyer with the coupon on it and stormed out.

Seven blocks of angry speed walking later, Arnold found the clown outside on the street still handing out flyers to the poor unknowing masses that what he was offering was not universal. He walked straight up to the white face painted mascot and slapped the stack of flyers from his hand.

"What is this?" Arnold held the flyer up to the Clown.

"A flyer for a free cheeseburger, Sir." The Clown said with a shakiness in his voice as he tried to bend over and pick up the flyers.

"No. No, this is the bullshit franchise system that allows individually operated stores to pick and choose the promotions they offer causing hard working men and women like me to make fools of themselves when they try to simply get a free sandwich from a store too cheap to participate as if consistency among a brand isn't a thing anymore!"

"I'm sorry, Sir. I just hand out the flyers. I don't make the rules. If you like I can talk to my manager and see what we can do to make this right. Or you could just use the coupon here since you're standing in front of a participating store now."

"Tell your manager this!" Arnold shoved the flyer into the clown's mouth leaving a bit of it still poking out, which he proceeded to punch the rest of the way in. Blood sprayed from the Clown's nose and his bright red honker turned into a deviated septum. The Clown was on the pavement and Arnold straddled him while bystanders looked on in shock. The store's staff had crowded around the entrance, but no one came to the Clown's aid. Soon it was hard to tell where the Clown's makeup ended, and the blood began.

Wayne's Manner

"I got aggravated assault because children were watching me the entire time." Arnold slammed back his shot. "And I was admittedly aggravated."

Wayne took his shot slowly. "Clowns are stupid anyway."

"It actually may have saved my life. It started me on a better path. The rest of these tattoos tell that story."

"Please, continue." Wayne leaned in.

"No, my turn." Ricky lined up another round as Arnold turned to Wayne. "Why are you here?"

"I just told you. Boring bar for a boring guy."

"But that's not why you're in Texas. You're not from here. That's clear. Why are you here?" Arnold sipped his beer.

Feeling a bit pressured by Arnold's change in body language and change in drinking habit during this volley of questioning, Wayne took a deep drink and searched for the words in his head. "My parents were killed here." Wayne drank some more. "We were driving home from visiting a friend of my Dads who was turning thirty-five or forty or something. I'm not sure. Haven't seen or heard from that person since."

Wayne's parent's brand-new Nissan Maxima pulled out of the driveway of his Dad's friend's house. The friend and his wife's faces were blurred in Wayne's memory and it made them look like witnesses of a crime trying to stay anonymous. The world around Wayne moved past via glimpses of trees, other cars, and soon buildings as he focused his attention on his Nintendo Game Boy. He was determined to beat the special Pokémon Yellow edition he had gotten only a few months earlier at Christmas, before they made it home. It was a four-hour drive and he was awfully close to the end. He planned to make easy work of the final gym and be crowned the very best.

Conversation with his old friend had let time get away from him as these things are like to do and it landed them dead stop in Dallas five-o'clock traffic. Nothing was moving. For all the lanes and twisting and turning stacks of highway the commuting population of Dallas still managed to jam itself up. Wayne really didn't notice. He was eight and his only concern was if his line-up of Pokémon were well trained enough. Wayne's Dad had made this trip several times before on his own and with Wayne's mom before Wayne was born so he knew some secret ways to get around the gridlock. There was an exit coming up which he knew he could use to circumvent a great deal of the bumper-to-bumper madness they now faced. It only took about fifteen minutes to reach the exit that very few people were taking because on the surface it appeared to only spill out into an industrial area filled with warehouses and factories. Wayne's Dad smiled back at him and then turned his attention back to the road and took the exit. They had barely breached the outside of the vein of cars when they were struck by a truck at seventy miles per hour that was driving along the shoulder.

The truck took out the entire front end of the luxury family sedan leaving only the backseat in near untouched condition. Wayne was knocked unconscious and wouldn't learn of his parent's death for three days. A family friend took him in so he wouldn't have to suffer the struggles of the foster care system.

"I come back every year on the anniversary of their death. Makes me feel close to them still. However, I still have not beaten that game."

"You should have gone first." Arnold held his shot up and waited for Wayne. "That way my funny story about beating up a clown would have lightened the mood." Wayne lifted his drink up as well and Arnold clinked them together. "To your parents." This made Wayne smile. "Whoa," Arnold looked around, "you don't want to be smiling in this place. Just take the shot."

Chapter 23

The curtains were pulled and the master bedroom was a hospitable zone for a vampire as Wayne sat in the corner on a chair he honestly tried six times before sitting in to ensure it wouldn't affect the world around him except his comfort. It had been years since Wayne watched someone die and even those thoughts were only memories planted in his head by the EMTS who explained what had happened to his parents. Mrs. Fairweather was expected, but still difficult to handle and then now he was witness to the horrible fiery death of Mr. Fairweather. Fire and water before coming to this place were for washing, cooking, heat, and cleaning, but now it was all about death and danger. Strangely his mind began to wander to a video game he had not beaten yet and at least three movies he'd planned on seeing. Simple things of his old life that were way less heavy than his new one.

A soft knock wrapped at the door and it opened slowly. Wayne thought for a moment how rude it was but didn't really care. Josie tiptoed in. Her innocence echoed through every crack of the wood floors.

"Are you okay?" Josie loudly whispered.

"I'm always okay." Wayne uttered.

"Okay," Josie crept in further. "Real quick, where are you?"

Click! A lamp illuminated Wayne's location. "Holy Otis!" Josie jumped back exactly two and a half feet. She counted it in her head. "I'm not sure why, but I expected you to be standing right in front of me."

"And you were scared I wasn't?"
"Duh! Dork. Expectation is never as scary as surprise."
"Thanks, Wes Craven."
"Who?"
"Please, don't." Wayne stood up and crossed the room, but as he did, he realized he wasn't going anywhere and was only crossing because it was more dramatic than to remain sitting. "I'm not too sure I'm fit for this life. I mean, sure I'm now a massive hero and can make phone calls from anywhere in existence, but maybe playing video games and watching paint dry is my calling."

"Where is this coming from? You have untold wealth, an executive chef on call, a butler, a maid, and an angry groundskeeper and you think you should be home in a dingy apartment playing video games on your beer stained recliner?" Josie stared blankly at Wayne.

"How did you know my recliner was beer stained?"
"It wasn't a difficult guess." Josie cracked a quick smile. "Kidding." She remarked after with a playful tone that screamed, she wasn't kidding.

"Seeing what happened to Mr. Fairweather just freaked me out a bit." Wayne shrugged. Josie crossed over to him. She looked around his head and poked him on the nose. "Ouch! What was that for?"

"Just being weird while I thought about exactly what I wanted to say." Josie hopped like a rabbit and danced around the room for a second before turning back to Wayne. "You said that you saw what happened through a photograph that was a combination of the memories of the people in it. Right?"

"Right."
"But Mr. F wasn't in the photo. Right?"
"Right."
"So, maybe you don't know the full story yet."

"And you're saying, what?"

"You're just being stubborn to waste time and words and drag this whole thing out, aren't ya?"

"Yeah, pretty much."

"You need to get in that room and figure it out!" Josie grabbed his shoulders. "I saw the way you looked at that door. There is something in you that needs to get in there. So, do it."

Wayne looked down at the part of his arm where the tattoo he got after meeting Arnold was. "Will you help me?"

"No." Josie pulled a comb and a piece of gum out of her pocket. Removed the wrapper. Stuck the dry stick of gum behind her ear like a cigarette and folded the wrapper over the comb and played it like a kazoo.

"Oh, okay."

"Psyche! Of course, I'll help, dumb dumb. I always help." She stuck her DIY instrument in her pocket and pulled the stick of gum from behind her ear.

"Awesome thank you."

"On one condition." She popped the gum into her mouth and began to chew big long chews as she strutted over to Wayne as if she was some sort of high fashion gangster.

"Great. What is it?"

Josie walked around Wayne, looking him up and down. When she returned to his front, she blew a big bubble and popped it herself then said, "You have to wear whatever I say to the party."

"Fine. Deal."

"Yay!" Josie's persona instantly reverted to herself, "But it's starting soon so let's get you dressed!" She smacked his butt as she walked out. "We'll discuss you disappearing on me earlier, later." She yelled back. "Like later we'll talk about what happened earlier. When you disappeared!"

"I'm right here." Wayne said while walking right beside Josie.

Ginger and Josie stood side by side. Josie's hands were held to her mouth almost as if in prayer while Ginger rested her right elbow in her left hand and slowly caressed her own cheek with her forefinger. They both stared straight forward.

"I don't know guys." Wayne stood before them wearing an incredibly well fitted suit with his arms awkwardly out to the side. "I mean, blue?" His suit was a dark blue jacket with a medium grey pant. The jacket was a two button with a slightly silky lapel.

"I love it!" Josie clapped her hands and jumped up and down.

"I'd find a reason to take it off you." Ginger bit her lip. "And that's a good thing."

Wayne took a good look at Ginger and knew it was her but couldn't determine if she was that much older than Josie now as they stood side by side.

"Okay, thanks?" Wayne brushed his hands over the expensive suit. "But what if I spill on it?"

"Oh, my dear, I can get any stain out of anything. And I mean any stain." Ginger winked.

"Okay, I'd like to take this off now." Wayne unbuttoned the one button that was buttoned because with a two-button jacket Josie had informed him you only button one button. He peeled the jacket halfway off his shoulders revealing a very festive and Moroccan inspired lining.

Josie lunged toward him and pulled it back on. "No! Remember our deal!" She buttoned the one button one that was supposed to be buttoned.

"Fine." Wayne adjusted his shoulders and settled into the weird feeling of wearing a suit. "But no tie."

Wayne's Manner

"Sweetheart, this is a party. The only person who will be wearing a tie here tonight is the President." Ginger bent over and picked up a laundry basket making sure to show off her cleavage in the process. Wayne could not help but look.

"Ehmmm. My eyes are over here." Josie redirected Wayne's stare to her face.

"Did she just say President? As in, Of the United States?" Wayne whispered to Josie as to not sound like an idiot in front of Ginger whom he was starting to develop a small crush on.

"Yeah. Mr. and Mrs. Fairweather have always donated tons of money to Government programs that support the arts and sciences because of how important those things are to the future and wellbeing of humanity. However, they only invite Presidents who also support the arts and sciences." Josie looked away from Wayne and gave a wink to nobody.

"Who did you just wink at?" Wayne looked around.

Josie found her reflection in an adjacent mirror. "Myself." She winked again. "Come on. You have the suit on. Now let's go to the library and do your thing."

Ginger held the laundry basket with one arm and adjusted her top. "My dears, whatever it is you're doing make sure you get it done quick like. The guests will be arriving in an hour." She turned and walked out of the room still fluffing her breast into a perfect presentation.

"Is it just me or does Ginger look about fifty years younger?" Wayne asked Josie as he watched Ginger's curvy hips leave the room.

"Men. It's all about looks with your kind." Josie turned and walked out of the room after Ginger. Wayne caught himself checking her out as well.

"What is wrong with me?" He took a few steps toward the door when he heard a slight clunk and what sounded like wind blowing through a crack. He turned and scanned the room but saw nothing except old suits and a closed window. Chalking it up to old house sounds, he shrugged it off and went to meet Josie in the library.

Chapter 24

Josie wrangled a stack of photo albums and plopped them down in front of Wayne who was feverishly flipping through pages of the Fairweather's memories.

"You're telling me you can just touch these photos and transport into the memory?"

"Yes."

"Way cool."

"But since real time passes while I'm in a memory we have to be quick and smart about which memories we visit. Wouldn't want to be late to greet the President...and the other guests." Wayne skipped past birthdays, game nights, and even several weddings for what appeared to be both Hollywood royalty and actual Royalty.

Josie took a different approach. She discounted entire albums based on their year and label. Albums labeled Cairo, Thailand, Australian Outback, and Outback Steakhouse were tossed aside reluctantly.

"There are so many pictures. Why do people take so many pictures?" Wayne slammed an album on the table stirring up dust and shaking some photos loose from their pages. "Why can't these just be digital and work with some sort of VR headset?"

"A what?" Josie asked without looking up from her mundane and depressing process of eliminating possible chances to visit some of the world's most incredible places just so Wayne could find his way into a den in the very house they were currently inside.

"Virtual Reality. You haven't heard of it?"

"Why would you want virtual reality when you can have reality reality?"

"The same reason you're looking at those photo albums wishing you could instantly jump anywhere in the world from right where you are."

"No offence, but that might have been the most insightful thing you've said since you've been here." Josie's mood shifted and the glint of adventure and excitement came back. "Thank you. I would much rather actually visit these places rather than hop into some picture of a memory I didn't make."

"That wasn't the point I was trying to make."

"But wasn't it?"

"Let's get back to work, we have thirty minutes before the first guests arrive." Wayne paused and choked on something inside his throat.

"Are you okay?" Josie asked with a puzzled look.

"Yeah, I just threw up a bit in my mouth after hearing myself concerned with being punctual."

"Gross. Please don't try to kiss me again."

"It wasn't a kiss!"

"Gotcha."

"Okay, great. You're one of those passive aggressive types who says things like, 'I see,' when someone is just answering the question you asked honestly. Perfect. Only person around my age for miles and she is just the worse. Well, I guess Ginger is looking rather good. I could get over the age gap for a woman like that." Wayne joked.

"No, I got the album!" Josie dusts off an album labeled 'Family Memories' and holds it up to Wayne.

"Oh. How do you know that's the one?" Wayne shook his head and continued to flip through the album in front of him that contained mostly pictures of various areas of the property including the former Ever Burning Forest, the Graveyard, as well as some strange ruins, caves, and a very large lake with boats on it that seemed to hover just above the water. "Now that seems unnecessary."

"Family memories will show us all sorts of photos from around the house that will probably include pictures of Mr. and Mrs. Fairweather. With that being the case one of them might lead us to a way in!" Josie cracked open the album and inside she found photos of the Fairweather's at a party in the house, their wedding in front of the Great Pyramids of Cairo, and an incredible amount of photos of a little Scottie dog sitting, laying, eating, drinking, licking, scratching, looking at the camera, looking at the camera with his tongue out, looking at the camera panting, looking away from the camera at something, blurred and running toward the something he saw, his butt as he ran away, and finally rubbing his back in the grass where something must have just been. "This has to be it."

"Why do you say that?"

"Just come here and don't make me fill the room with ridiculous exposition in order to guide you toward an action we all know you'll do anyway." Josie retorted.

The light that peered in from the hallway got darker and a shadow was cast over the photo. Wayne and Josie looked up and saw Morese standing patiently with his arms crossed behind his back.

"Yes, Morese?" Wayne asked with a bit of an attitude.

"Your guests are arriving, Sir. It would be quite rude to keep them waiting without their host."

"Isn't there like a special time in the night where you introduce me to everyone from the top of the stairs?"

"This isn't a debutante ball, Sir. Your latest adventure down someone else's memory lane can wait. Whatever it is you think is in that room will be there when the party's over. Trust me. It has been for almost forty years."

Reverting to a teenage boy for a moment, Wayne let out a short forceful huff in protest and leaned over the table placing both hands down flat, however, one missed the table and landed on a photo. The next thing Wayne knew he was standing in the desert looking up at the Great Pyramids and the Fairweathers or soon to be Fairweathers getting married.

"Son of a bitch." Wayne had already begun to sweat. "Take me home. Now!"

Wayne came back to life in the library and without missing a beat pushed all the other albums aside making it so the album Josie just brought out sat alone and unbothered by anything else.

"Sir, what on Earth are you doing?" Morese sounded genuinely annoyed for the first time since Wayne had arrived.

"Isolating this album so I remember which one it is."

"That's cute." Josie straightened Wayne's jacket and made sure the single button was firmly buttoned.

"Why is this cute?"

"No one else is going to touch these albums. It is clearly labeled what it is and what I just said it was."

"Don't toss logic at me. Not right now."

Josie put her finger over Wayne's lips, pressing in a bit too hard when she did. "Now, go make your debut Mr. Morris." Josie led Wayne out of the library. Wayne paused at the doorway and shook sand from his shoes onto the clean rug. He watched it drool out with curiosity.

Chapter 25

The floorboards rattled and vocalized their irritation under Wayne's feet. The long runners absorbed each step as if made of Jell-O. Wayne liked Jell-O. He particularly enjoyed the kind with a little bit of cream swirl. His mom used to pack some in his lunch every day. He was standing at the top of the stairs when his thoughts returned from his journey down Jell-O memory lane and he watched as Morese, ahead of him and already at the door as usual, turned the giant knob and pulled it open. A flood of people slid through the entry wearing all sorts of fancy clothing. His suit now felt like cardboard stained with blueberry jam. Far from fashion forward. However, without knowing a thing about fashion Wayne wasn't sure if cardboard covered in jam had a chance of being the next hit craze.

The first couple through the door wore sashes and crowns. Perfect, let's set the stage high right out of the gate. "Prince Ahmose I and Princess Nefertari of Egypt." Morese announced as the couple made their way inside and were greeted by Ginger holding a tray of champagne flutes complete with bubbly. Wayne didn't even know Egypt still had royals. "Professor Tennessee Smith of the University of Arizona." The same process for the Egyptian royalty was repeated with the professor who turned down the champagne and made his way to the bar cart where to Wayne's surprise O'Connor was set up in a tux tending bar. O'Connor poured the Professor a double whiskey neat without either man exchanging words.

They've clearly done this before a time or two. A third couple came through both in dress blues and both highly decorated. "Lieutenant Colonel Jessica Callaway and Major Richard Callaway of the United States Marine Corps." The decorated husband and wife also declined the champagne and made their way to a respectable area of the room where they stood and waited for the rest of the guests to arrive.

Group after group came through the door and the names and affiliations blurred past Wayne's attention like a stock car at Daytona. Before he knew it he was shoulder deep in a sea of unknown faces with all their eyes on him, the Fresh Prince of Ramble Ridge. With anxiety levels increasing Wayne searched for a familiar face, however, to his misfortune he was not even able to find Morese, Ginger, or Josie in the mix. His guests were from all walks of life, but all carried a weight of intrigue about them. Whether it be something about their clothing such as the couple from Zimbabwe or the two men who looked like they just stepped off the set of a modern day Miami Vice, or the cheap parlor tricks being performed by a man with a scarf covering half of his face diagonally, each person seemed to have a story waiting to be asked about. Wayne desperately desired to engage these people more than simply, "Hi, how are you," but his social skills only went as far as one or maybe two people. What he needed was Josie, but she had disappeared.

As if hiding it from the teacher during a test, Wayne pulled his phone from his pocket and sent a low-key text to Josie, "Where are you?"

"This is a beautiful party. The Fairweathers would be proud."

Wayne jerked his head up and nervously stuffed the phone back into his pocket in a strange force of habit and noticed Prince Ahmose I and Princess Nefertari standing before him with the most perfect posture he had ever seen. "Or I should say Mrs. Fairweather would." Prince Ahmose I corrected himself. "We never had the honor of meeting Mr. Fairweather. However, my father was at their wedding and he tells me it was simply beautiful."

"It was." Wayne blurted out before he could think about how crazy that sounded. "I mean, I've seen pictures."

"Oh, you must show us sometime. Ahmose and I were married at the same spot and I would just die to see it." Princess Nefertari ecstatically requested.

"Oh, I can do more than show you." Wayne bit his own lip and shook his head. "Why do you keep doing that?" He muttered under his breath.

"Doing what?" Prince Ahmose leaned in to hear him better.

"Umm," There was a break in the crowd and Wayne saw O'Connor pour whiskey into a glass. "I'm sorry. My bartender is over pouring, again!" Wayne nervously made his way over to the bar. The Prince and Princess looked at each other very confused. "It's not like a money thing." Wayne stumbled both over his words and his feet on his way. "It's a safety thing. You get it!" He reached the bar and turned his back to his guests. "Whiskey. Rocks. Over pour that shit."

"Bit o'social anxiety, eh?" O'Connor poured Wayne a drink three fingers high. "Aren't you the boyo who just defeated a bear who was entirely engulfed in flames?" He slid the drink over to Wayne.

"This is different. There's no magic chair to make all of this more comfortable." Wayne took a big sip. "And he wasn't entirely covered. Just like the shoulder area."

"I think the magic chair you seek is in your hand." O'Connor wiped down the bar top. "But I get what you mean. The only man here I somewhat respect is the Professor there. Party's only been going for forty-five minutes and the man is already on his third bevvy. That's a min you don't go shot for shot with. Unless you're me." O'Connor pulled a shooter of whiskey from under the bar and threw it back. That's for Big Yin!" O'Connor held his empty in the air toward the unnoticing Professor.

"Should you be drinking so much while working?" Wayne took another sip.

"Should you?" O'Connor gestured the likes of a baby suckling its mom's nipple. "Oan yer bike!" He set his shot glass upside down next to three others under the bar top as he ushered Wayne away. Wayne took his drink and scooted back as several other guests crowded the bar eager for refreshments.

Wayne reintegrated back into the horde of royalty, celebrity, and notables. His eye transfixed on the Professor. A familiarity shot out in all directions like shrapnel from an 'I know that guy' grenade. His palms dripped and sense memory of Prom night came rushing back. The Professor was Lindsay Matheney and Wayne was Wayne. However, instead of going over to ask her to dance he turned to Beth Lewis and wiggled nonsensical words from his lips that resembled an invitation through the deafening tunes of the late 2000's pop and R&B. In this case Beth Lewis took the form of Madame Claire Grimm, a tall and slender woman in a skintight satin dress whose edges could only be found by the change in color from red to the porcelain tone of her flawless skin. Towering at least a foot over Wayne's head her chest met his face and welcomed his stare with an open neckline. She was already a much better dance partner than Beth Lewis and he'd not even laid a hand on her.

"I could have been your mother." A soft and sultry voice whispered in Wayne's ear without Madame Grimm even leaning over as if carried by the air straight from her lips to him. After a moment of seduction shock Wayne registered what she said.

"Wait, what?"

"I'm old enough to be your mother." Madame Grimm's voice, although remaining smooth and pleasant, had lost a bit of its subtleness.

"Oh, yeah. I, um, didn't notice." Wayne averted his eyes from what now appeared to him as a completely inappropriate dress for such an event.

"But age is just a number." The soft backside of her hand slowly caressed his cheek. The other hand grabbed him and pulled him closer placing his left arm around her and positioning his hand on the small of her back.

"I gave at the office. I mean, I have a girlfriend?" Wayne tried to wiggle free, but Madame Grimm used the movement of his body to slide into a nice slow dance.

"You even look like him." Her arms wrapped around his back like vines strangling a chain link fence. She leaned her head onto his shoulder and nibbled at his ear. His wiggle shifted suddenly to a shake. His excitement was growing, and his only option was to pull her closer to conceal it like a middle schooler walking the hall to third period with a thick textbook held firmly to his lap. "Hello there, Mr. Morris."

"Like who?" He stuttered out. "I look like who?"

"Like Mr. Fairweather of course."

Wayne took this moment in her vulnerability and broke free. The shock was evident on his face. He'd been to the Fairweather's wedding through the pictures and he knew he didn't look like the man he saw in Egypt. Before the Madame could press the matter further, Ginger strode by wearing an attitude of ownership over young Wayne. "Sir, I'm sure your other guests are just dyin' to get to know you better. You might consider spreadin' the love a bit more." Her eyes shot barbed wire and pitchforks at Madame Grimm as Ginger ushered Wayne away. This confusion served to lower his excitement levels back to normal.

"That woman is trouble. Trust me. She's a liar." Ginger stuck close to Wayne's side, her bare arm rubbing the soft fabric of his suit jacket. "She may look beautiful, but her true form is downright shameful."

A waiter walked by with a plate of little smokies complete with fancy toothpicks stuck in their sides. A guest dressed to the nines in a Versace dress and a perfectly white pearl necklace grabbed one, "They say one can tell a lot about a man by the food he eats. Clearly our host is stuck somewhere between trailer park teenager and state college frat boy." She took a small bite of the smokie and attempted to chew. Gagging, she spat out the barely quarter of an inch piece into a napkin. Her date burst out laughing and it wasn't long before she was too.

"Ignore those pretentious folks, darling. They wouldn't know good home cookin' if it jumped up and bit them in the rear. Besides, those two are only here because they donated an entire wing to the Fairweather's museum a few years back. Money got them in here, not respect."

"Museum?"

"Another story for another day, my dear." Ginger stopped dead in her tracks and looked to the top of the stairs. "Now would you look at that? Seems the sun's risen indoors these days."

Wayne looked up with her and saw Josie in a brilliant pink fluffy strapless dress, her hair pulled up in curls like a fancy wedding cake, and all the nerves and anxiety that can fit into such a small person.

"Wow." Wayne let slip.

"Go get her, stud." Ginger nudged him with a slight hint of jealousy in her voice.

The sea of people split open as if by magic as Wayne approached the stairs. A million thoughts raced through his mind. Where did she get that dress? How did she do her hair like that alone? Why does the Professor look so familiar? Why

147

are we having a party in the grand entrance of the house and not in a ballroom? Probably because the ballroom is haunted or a gateway to a rundown K-Mart where the blue light specials are so good you shop till you drop. Which foot do I normally step with first when going up stairs? Before he knew it, he was face to face with Josie. "How did I make it up the stairs so fast?" His hand flew over his mouth when he realized the last question came out loud.

"You didn't." Josie blushed and laughed a bit. She looked down and Wayne followed her lead. They were at the bottom of the stairs. "You were standing there staring for what must have been five minutes, so I figured I better come down and make sure you were okay."

"It couldn't have been that long."

"Well, I don't think all your guests are standing there staring at me." Josie looked out past Wayne.

"Ha ha. Nice one. But if they were staring, I have no doubt it would be for you." Wayne smiled and looked up into her eyes that were still looking out past him into the crowd.

"That's sweet, but you should turn around."

Wayne turned to see every of one his guests facing him and staring with what seemed like genuine concern. "Hi, everybody. Everything is okay. Thanks for the awkward stares."

"Speech!" A voice echoed through the crowd.

"What was that?" Wayne looked around for the origin of the guest who seemed to be trying to make Wayne's embarrassment a much larger spectacle.

"I think the young master owes us all a speech." The guests, who were also looking for the heckler, made gaps and spaces between them until the only person with their back turned to Wayne was spotted standing by the bar. It was the Professor. He turned with a drink in his hand and looked directly at

Wayne. "You brought us all here. I personally would like to hear a speech."

Behind the Professor, O'Connor held up seven fingers and even mouthed the word "Seven" to Wayne.

"I'm not really one for speeches." Wayne backed up into the bottom step and fell backwards only to have Josie catch him and prop him back up just as fast as it happened.

"Come on, my boy. I don't care what you say. Just say something." The Professor took a long gulp of his whiskey never losing eye contact with Wayne. "Afterall. You are the mystery boy who just took over the Fairweather estate. None of us have a single clue as to who you are."

As if the rest of the guests hadn't really thought about it or they had and chose to ignore it because they didn't want to taint one of the biggest social engagements of the year, they all turned to one another and began to chatter and speculate as to who Wayne really was and why Mrs. Fairweather would give him everything.

The cells that made up Wayne's body shook and rattled. He wasn't prepared to say anything and had nothing to say. A hundred pairs of eyes took turns piercing his soul. Josie was rubbing his shoulders, but he didn't feel a thing.

"I'm okay!"

The room fell silent. Wayne again spoke aloud what he was trying to keep inside.

"I'll be right back." He darted up the stairs getting his foot tangled in Josie's dress causing one of his shoes to fall off. Not bothering to stop to retrieve it, Wayne continued up and then down the hall toward the library.

"Ladies and Gentlemen, our host, Cinderella." The Professor finished off his whiskey and before he could set it down O'Connor already had another pour going.

Chapter 26

The inaudible tone of the party conversation drifted through the halls. Darkness occupied the library except what little light peered through the doorway. Wayne was hunched over the table flipping through albums and placing his hand on almost every picture taken within the house.

"...to you!"

"And many more!" Morese sang out in a beautiful soprano voice. Ginger, O'Connor, Mrs. Fairweather, Mr. Fairweather, and Morese all stood with Morese around Santiago as he sat before a large birthday cake that was less than professional quality. Wayne watched from a low angle in the corner.

"Dios mio. You all are too pure to me. I think it is absolutely childlike that you made this cake yourselves." Santiago turned and embraced each person's hand with both of his in a very endearing way.

"Childlike! We do something nice for you and you insult us? That is awfully rude, young man." Ginger pulled her hand away from Santiago's.

"I believe he meant adorable or cute." Mr. Fairweather chimed in while relighting his cigar. "Santiago is still mastering our complicated and confusing language. He'll get it soon. We've been working on it each night in my study."

"I do hope so." Ginger's demeanor shifted from disgusted to flirtatious. "I also hope you stop getting older. Having you around has me feeling younger every day."

Wayne pulled his hand from the photo and placed it on another.

Now outside, Wayne was staring at a single rose growing in the garden. Mrs. Fairweather walked over to the rose and delicately held it in her hand and breathed in a long slow supply of the flower's scent. She turned to the camera and smiled. The flash crackled out and Wayne found himself back in the library again.

Over and over he touched photos.

"What do you call it?" A much younger Mrs. Fairweather leaned over the kitchen counter.

"Spaghetti cake." An equally younger Santiago grinned.

"You should workshop it."

Another one.

A twenty something Mr. Fairweather stands in front of a mirror wearing a genuinely nice three-piece suit holding the camera. Wayne stood next to him. From behind them both a soft and seductive voice rolled through the room.

"How about you get that suit down to as many pieces of clothing that I'm wearing?"

Mr. Fairweather and Wayne both turned around to see Mrs. Fairweather in lingerie only moments before she lifted the shoulder straps and dropped it to the ground. Wayne's hand shot up over his eyes.

Back in the library Wayne's hand quickly lifted from the photo and onto another one.

Josie poked her head around the edge of the doorway and watched for a moment. She could see Wayne move only briefly before being sucked into a near catatonic state.

He was now in the entryway as movers hauled in the giant carved door that now blocked his way into the study. Mr. Fairweather ushered them in.

"Right this way my boys. Be incredibly careful. That door holds a magic the likes you couldn't possibly understand."

The movers glanced at each other around the side of the door and snickered. "Sure, thing boss." One spouted with sarcastic authority.

"Wouldn't want to be pulling a rabbit out of my ass later." The other cracked.

"Very funny, Mr. Copperfield. No, this magic is far more curious than sleight of hand parlor tricks." Mr. Fairweather eyed the door with the same admiration he'd shown at his wedding to Mrs. F.

"Whatever, pal. Where do you want it?"

"Right over here." Mr. Fairweather led them over to the doorway of the study. Wayne barely got a glimpse inside before the movers walked in the way blocking his view. "Just bring it right up next to the threshold here."

"Listen, bud, we ain't installing this hunk of wood for you. We're just the movers. You know that, right?"

"Very much so. Just hold it right up there for just a moment." Mr. Fairweather ran around to the front of the door and focused his attention on the carving of a mermaid near the left side of the door. She was beautiful and very pronounced in all the usual places. The movers, starting to struggle from the weight of the door stared at him as if he had lost it.

"Hey man! This thing is heavy. You can ogle your little girlfriend there later."

Mr. Fairweather ignored the remark and closed his eyes and leaned in with his lips puckered and laid a big kiss on the rear end of the mermaid. Instantly the door was sucked out of the mover's hands and shot straight and snug into the doorway to the study.

"Holy hell!" The mover on the right froze.

"I'm outta here!" The mover on the left darted, grabbing the other mover on his way out the main door.

"Thanks for all your help, boys! I'll have a check in the mail tomorrow morning!" Mr. Fairweather hollered out while not taking his eyes off the door. He walked right up to the freshly and magically mounted door and grabbed the knob opening it without issue. Taking just a moment to admire the mystical precision of the installation, Mr. F left only enough of a gap and barely any time for Wayne to get a better look than before. All he could make out was a large desk with an old lamp on in, a brown leather chair, and some weird square door on the wall. Mr. F then headed inside, closing the door after him.

Wayne pulled his hand away from the photo. "Why can't I just get a break here?" He pushed the album away with force. It knocked into a stack of other albums and like a tower of Jenga blocks they crashed to the floor.

Josie made her way in inch by inch quietly and kneeled to pick them up. Her hands were sorting and stacking the albums, picking up any photos that had been shook loose, but her eyes were locked on Wayne.

"What?" The word came out of Wayne's mouth like a whip.

"Are you okay?"

"Does it seem like I'm okay?" It did not seem like he was okay.

"Was it what that drunk Professor guy said? Ignore him. He was just being a jerk for the sake of being a jerk."

"He's right though. Who am I to have all of this? Down there at the party are kings and queens, decorated Military, a woman who I'm pretty sure runs a brothel, and a Professor to name a few. Who am I? A guy who lucked into the craziest house ever?"

Josie stood and set the stack of albums on the table gently. Another stack of discarded photos fought her fingers as she tried to sort them into a nice neat stack. Sharp corners stabbed her fingers, but she paid no mind. "I hardly think you need to be jealous of a woman who owns a brothel."

A smile cracked across Wayne's face for a moment. "I don't know. I think owning my own brothel might be kind of great."

Josie clinched her fist and punched Wayne clean out of his chair sending him crashing to the floor. His foot kicked the underside of the table on the way down knocking the photos Josie just finished stacking back to the floor. "Dang it, Wayne! I just finished with those!"

"You're the one who punched me with the force of like a thousand men."

"I focus the majority of my experience points on attack."

Wayne crawled over to where the photos rested at Josie's feet. Fighting away the puffy pink skirt of her dress Wayne gathered the photos, however, he didn't even attempt to make them nice and neat. "How on Earth are we going to find out which of these photos go in which album?"

"Stop changing the subject. Now, put your shoe back on." Josie dropped Wayne's shoe to the ground beside him causing a loud thud which startled Wayne. He raised up and smacked his head on the table which echoed the thud the shoe made.

"For the love of…"

"Oh, come on! I haven't ever had to tell a man to get dressed so many times in one day."

Wayne peeled himself out from under the table and plopped his butt down on the floor scraping the lonely shoe over. "And just how many men have you had to tell to get dressed?"

Josie's face rushed red. "Well, none." She hurried toward the door. "Besides you." She walked out into the hall and out of sight. Wayne fixed his missing shoe problem with a bullshit grin on his face. Josie returned, "That's not the point though. Now, I believe I've done a sufficient job of distracting you from your worries so I think it would be fitting for you to escort me back to the party of which I haven't been able to enjoy one minute of and I really want to dance!" She presented her hand to Wayne. He glanced at the mess of stacked photos on the floor beside him then back to Josie with a smile.

"How chivalrous of you to help a weak little lady like myself in such a way. I do believe you're right. I do owe you a dance." Wayne took her hand and stood up. On the way up he grabbed the stack of photos and snuck them into his jacket pocket.

"After you."

Chapter 27

The tray of little smokies was nearly full when Wayne first stopped the waiter. Now only a few remained.

"Would you like me to go to the kitchen and get another tray, Sir?" The Waiter asked doing the best he could to not sound too judgmental.

"Yes!" Wayne spoke through two half chewed barbeque glazed miniature wieners.

"No." Josie pulled Wayne away from the poor waiter who'd been standing there with his arm up for nearly ten minutes.

A long loud breath erupted from the Waiter's mouth as he gripped the arm, he had been holding the tray with. His whole body nearly sank to the ground as he sulked away, unsure if he was supposed to return with another tray of weaners. This would haunt him the rest of his life.

"You need to mingle." Josie guided him through the crowd. They passed a man with a scar straight down the center of his left eye.

"Hi!" Wayne reached out his hand to the man.

"Nope, not him." She pulled his hand back and smiled at the scarred man. "We're all pretty sure he killed his brother on a safari trip in Africa."

"What?" Wayne looked back at the scarred man in terror. "Why is he here then?"

"They couldn't prove it. His nephew was the only witness and he's been missing ever since."

"Well, I would rather murderers not be in my house. Like, for next time."

They came upon two individuals with their backs turned to them. "Here, I don't think they've killed anyone." Josie ushered Wayne forward.

"How can you tell? We're looking at the back of their heads." Wayne griped at Josie.

"Well, I suppose it would be pretty easy for me to get away with it." One of the men turned around. He looked as if he stepped right out of one of the men's fashion and lifestyle magazines Wayne got free for several years in exchange for airline points, he received as payment once. The lighting in the room seemed to hit the man's features perfectly.

"Why? Because you're the most handsome man alive?" Wayne blurted out in awe.

"No, he'd just try to pin it on me." The man next to him turned around. He looked as if he stepped right out of one of the men's fashion and lifestyle magazines Wayne got free for several years in exchange for airline points, he received as payment once. The lighting in the room seemed to hit the man's features perfectly.

"Holy twins!"

"Or the both of you would come up with an elaborate plan to pin it on me." A third man popped his head between the first two men and draped his arms around their shoulders. He looked as if he stepped right out of one of the men's fashion and lifestyle magazines Wayne got free for several years in exchange for airline points, he received as payment once. The lighting in the room seemed to hit the man's features perfectly.

"All three of you can pin whatever you want to me." Josie uttered in a daze. Wayne whipped his head around to her.

"You've been spending too much time with Ginger." He turned back to the triplets. "So, there are three men who were a thousand times luckier than I was."

"I don't know, look around." Triplet One said.

"Pretty sweet digs if you ask me." Triplet Two said.

"You got any spare rooms?" Triplet Three asked.

"I mean in the looks department. Besides, you all are probably princes, or explorers, or you work with Doctors Without Borders and in your free time save puppies and kittens with your shirts off."

"No, actually none of those." Triplet Two said.

"Really?"

"Yeah, we're just pretty normal guys." Triplet One said.

"Thank God."

"Yeah, we're just teachers." Triplet Three said.

"What kind of teaching do you do?"

"Special needs." All three men spoke at once.

"Son of a --"

"And in our free time we dress up as superheroes and visit children's hospitals." Triplet One added.

"I think I'd like to talk to Scar Man over there now." Wayne dug at Josie.

"Phillip, Phillip, Phillip." Professor Smith strolled over to Wayne, Josie, and the Triplets. "Or should I say, Phillip, Phillip, and Phillip. That's no way to treat our gracious host. Pull yourself together. Show some respect." The way he lifted his whiskey glass to his lips commanded great power and the triplets all hung their heads at the same time then magically they all blended into one single person.

"Whoa. What? How?" Wayne stumbled back bumping into a distinguished looking man in a top hat. "So, sorry. They just...three...into...did you just see that?" The man in the top hat scoffed rather pretentiously and turned back to his conversation. Wayne, refocusing on the Professor and a now single human named Phillip, "You should tell that guy to show respect." Wayne emphasized 'that.' "Actually, don't. I don't want him to turn into a giant peanut or something."

"I'm not sure which is cooler? That you were triplets or that you can be triplets if you want to be. Probably the latter. Just imagine what I could do if I could split into three." Josie jumped side to side quickly pretending to be more than one person.

"Sounds like there already are two of you the way you both ramble on so much." The Professor quipped.

"How do you do that? Um…"

"Phillip."

"Phillip." Wayne reached out to shake his hand.

"I'm not actually three people. It's this totem here. It allows me to project up to three versions of me at the same time. Comes in real handy when I need a good wingman." Phillip pulled a necklace up from his shirt and showed Wayne and Josie. The chain was silver and led down to a triangle medallion with three different colored stones inlaid in the center. One red, one blue, and one green. "The Professor here actually helped me understand it after I found it in a box of things my grandfather left me when he passed."

"Thank you, Phillip for the lovely exposition of your life. I'm sure that information will be very useful to the young Master Wayne at a later date." The Professor reached his drinking hand out and set the glass down on a passing waiter's tray and subsequently grabbed a new one from the tray of a different waiter passing the other direction. It was like synchronized drinking.

"Yes, you're right, Sir. If you'll excuse me." Phillip bowed a little and as he rose, he split into three again, but remained in one place, each head of himself winking at Josie on the way up into yet again one solid Phillip. Then he walked away.

"You'll have to excuse Phillip. This is all very new to him. As I'm sure it is with you."

"I'm really trying not to be surprised by anything, but it seems literally impossible."

"You need a drink. Or possibly seven if you're going to catch up with me."

"Oh, I don't think I need to catch up with you. I don't drink that much. One will be fine."

"If you want my help, you'll go drink for drink with me." The Professor turned to O'Connor who was across the room still tending the bar and raised his glass to his lips after which O'Connor rapidly began pouring a tray of shots.

Wayne stared at the Professor a moment trying to process him. He seemed so familiar, but he was sure they'd never met.

The Professor, still not looking at Wayne, finished his drink and held the empty glass out in front of him, examining the detail of the crystal. "You don't remember me, do you?" In that moment, the Professor's shirt sleeve fell a bit revealing a few tattoos of upside-down capital T's with zig zagging lines moving up to a point. The Professor looked at Wayne and pulled his sleeve back up.

"Arnold!" Wayne's eyes grew three times the size of his head or at least that's how he pictured it in his mind.

"Professor Arnold 'Tennessee' Smith. Pleasure to make your re-acquaintance." Arnold offered his hand to a quite bewildered Wayne.

Chapter 28

"What are you doing here?" Wayne pulled Arnold over to the bar and looked around in concern and confusion.

"I feel I could ask you the same question." Arnold pulled up a stool near the temporary bar.

"To be honest. I'm still trying to figure that out myself." Wayne sat beside him and Arnold slid him a shot. Josie lingered off Wayne's right shoulder, shyly. She stared off at the ceiling as if extremely interested and intrigued by something up there.

"My apologies. I'm Arnold. An old friend of Wayne's." Arnold ushered for Josie to come closer. She did the whole 'who me' song and dance, trying not to be visibly excited to meet one of Wayne's friends. Arnold took her hand and gave it a kiss. "You must be the Misses."

"HA! Oh no! Me? Mrs. Morris? Never. I couldn't. I mean. Hi." Josie rushed back over to the other side of Wayne.

"Now that we've established that." Arnold indicated for another shot to be placed before Josie. "Let's drink." The three awkwardly brought their glasses together. They struggled at the moment of contact and ended up not all tapping each other at the same time.

Cheers. Oh. Oops. Okay. Cheers. Cheers was the general exchange that was made.

Arnold and Wayne took their shots with ease while Josie only took a sip. "Excuse me, O'Connor? Could I have some water to follow this with?"

"Of course." O'Connor cracked a bottle of water and poured her a sizable portion.

"Just like old times." Arnold cracked a glint of a smile.

"With much less dangerous of a crowd." Wayne chimed in.

"I wouldn't be so sure about that." Arnold looked around the room. The look on his face as he scanned the room was new to Wayne. Arnold was much more at ease at the Sunray Saloon and seemed to drink a little less there as well.

"So, Arnold. What are you doing here?" Wayne broke the tension the best way he knew how, with small talk.

"Well, there's a bit of my life I didn't share with you back then. Actually, quite a bit of it if I'm finally being honest with you."

"Can we start with when you became a Professor all of a sudden?" Wayne shook his glass around and up in some attempt to pantomime 'All of a sudden' using his drinking hand.

"Truth is, I always was. That job I lost, Yale. The boss who fired me, the Dean."

"Heavy." Wayne brought his drink back to a normal pose and sipped it awkwardly.

"Looks like you got back into it though, right?" Josie poked in. Always the bit of light that peeks through the cracks.

"Eventually, a bit after we'd met, I was given a second chance at the school I left for more ivy-covered walls. The University of Arizona."

"School, is that how you know the Fairweathers?" Wayne's mind was still trying to connect all the dots before he even had all the dots to begin with.

"You could say that."

"Well, I did. Is that the truth?"

"Why, haven't you gotten a bit more confident?"

"I fought a fire bear."

"That'll do it." Arnold took a drink. "You see that mask over there in the case by the stairs?" With drink in hand he pointed to a wooden mask with gold metal edges around the outside, the eyes, and the mouth. "Ol' Fairweather hired me to help him find that."

"What's it do?"

"Nothing. It's a mask. Covers your face. What else would it do?"

"Well Philip…"

"I'm messing with you. The wearer appears to be a tree to everyone else."

Wayne and Josie gave each other incredibly disappointed looks and at the same time uttered, "Oh."

"So, you feeling nostalgic?"

"What? You wanting to start a bar fight?" Wayne joked.

"No, why would I want to do that? Especially here. Have Philip triple team me or worse, those black ops fellas over there take me out before I could blink. No thank you. I was referring to the photos in your pocket." Arnold gestured down to the stack of photos peeking out of Wayne's jacket pocket.

"You took some with you?" Josie squawked. The sound she made resembled that of a dog toy.

"Yeah, sorry. Arnold, there is a room past that very ornate door, but I'm told I can't go in there. Also, the door is magically sealed shut so I couldn't even if I was allowed."

"And you naturally want to get in there even more because you're not allowed."

"Sort of."

"I get it. Reminds me of Cairo." Arnold glanced over at the Prince and Princess. "What's with the photos then?"

"They take you to a collective memory of the event captured. I…we…were thinking there might be a clue as to how to get inside."

"Let me see."

Wayne pulled the stack of photos from his pocket and handed them to Arnold. "Be careful. If you place your palm flat on the image, you'll be transported into the photo."

"Thanks for the heads up." Arnold sorted through the photos. A few of them were just shots of Mr. and Mrs. Fairweather, some of the garden, and one of a dead rabbit being consumed by maggots. "Who took these?"

"I think different people, but Ginger, the maid, seems to have been very interested in the camera. So maybe her."

Arnold slid the picture of the dead rabbit over to Wayne. "You think Ginger, that incredibly beautiful young woman over there," he looked over at Ginger bringing drinks to some of the guests and gave her a wink, "you think she took a picture of a decomposing dead rabbit?"

"Well, I did say other people were taking photos. Maybe."

"Yeah, you need to shift your perspective." Arnold's attention was still focused on Ginger who flirted with him from afar.

"How is finding who took these photos going to help? It could be anyone or several anyone's."

"All I'm saying is you seem to be looking at what they were taking the photo of and not who took the photo, or where from for that matter." Arnold stood up.

"Where are you going?"

"I have my own mystery to solve." Arnold downed his drink. "Shift your perspective, kid. Might surprise you." He patted Wayne on the back and walked away toward a blushing Ginger.

Wayne watched his mentor leave him. Josie grabbed the photos and pulled them closer to her.

"What does he mean?" Josie scattered the photos out on the bar.

"I don't know." Wayne watched Arnold start to dance a bit to the music. A groovy tune played resembling some Roadhouse Blues. Arnold was close to Ginger now and danced down into a squatting position, brought both his hands up to his eyes and mimed holding a camera pointed right at Ginger. One flick of his right index finger and Arnold had himself a mental snapshot of the beautiful woman. He pulled on the "edge" of the camera as if developing a polaroid then turned to Wayne, shook the photo, then tossed it to the confused master of the house accompanied by a wink only a cool dude like Arnold could pull off. Or Tennessee Smith.

Wayne imagined the photo landing at his feet and glanced back up to Arnold who was moving back up to an upright stance. "Wait." Wayne spun around on his stool and stole the photos from Josie. "Shift your perspective." As he flipped through the stack, he noticed something. Most of the photos were taken from a low angle. "Someone short took these."

"What?" Josie looked at the photos.

"Someone short took these photos. There is someone in these memories we are not seeing because they're not 'IN' the photos."

"How does that help?"

"I don't know." Wayne went through his stack again. He laid them all out on the bar top. From the random selection he'd taken there were several from a low angle of Mr. and Mrs. Fairweather dressed nicely as if they were heading off to some event in the big closet upstairs where Wayne had gotten his own suit. "There has to be something here."

"Maybe they set the camera on the floor?" Josie suggested. "They are alone in the closet." She lingered over the photos absorbing all the detail she could. "Oh! Or maybe they really like the way they look from low angles and had Ginger get down on her knees for the shot!"

"Let's not talk about Ginger being down on her knees, please."

Wayne isolated all the photos from the closet room. "Was there an album labeled 'Closet Photos' or something?"

"Yeah." Josie said seriously.

"Why?"

"Why not? Dressing up is fun!" Josie stepped away and spun around sending her dress into a whirl. "I have a whole album in my phone dedicated to my daily outfit."

"That's strange." Wayne said.

"Hey! I don't make fun of the things you like." Josie stomped. "Mr. Watches Paint Dry."

"No, not that. This one is taken in the closet room, but it is of the whole crew. Morese, Santiago, O'Connor, Mr. and Mrs. F, and Ginger!" Wayne pulled the photo and held it up. "Someone else took this photo!"

"But who?"

"I'll find out." Wayne reached out for the photo and Josie grabbed his wrist.

"No. Not here. You'll go catatonic in front of everyone and then they'll really think you're crazy."

"You're right. Come with me." Wayne scooped up the photos in his left hand and Josie in his right and they rushed off up the main stairs.

Prince Ahmose I and Princess Nefertari watched them as they went.

"They could be a bit more discreet." Princess Nefertari judged.

Lieutenant Colonel Jessica Callaway and Major Richard Callaway approached the royal couple.

"I think it's romantic." Lieutenant Colonel Callaway gushed.

"You would, Jessica." The Princess jabbed.

"That's Lieutenant Colonel, Neffy." Callaway retorted.

Major Callaway and Prince Ahmose glanced at each other and rolled their eyes.

Chapter 29

"Are you going to touch it?" Josie nudged Wayne.

Wayne stood still with the photo of the gang. Mr. Fairweather with his hair perfectly slicked back, suit pressed and fitted exactly right to his body, even his smile seemed tailor made. Mrs. Fairweather was a knockout and styled before her time in a tight black dress with one strap and an elegant brooch, that was fashioned to resemble a sunflower, pinned on. The staff were also dressed up. The men in tuxedos and Ginger in a less tight dress than Mrs. F, but still cut to show off what she has.

"Well?" Josie's gaze shifted to the photo.

"I don't think so."

"What?"

"I don't think I'm going to touch this photo. I don't think I'm going to see where it leads me." Wayne tapped the photo on his left hand.

"You've got to be kidding me." Josie stepped back. "After all this? The back and forth. The desperate desire to get into that room and you're not going to follow through? Wayne Morris you're killing me! This is like refusing the call to adventure, but way too late in the story making it all just seem so," Josie struggled to get her next word out, "pointless!"

Wayne looked up at Josie. His eyes were probably the sincerest they'd been since he arrived. He reached out his left hand to her and a slight smile broke across his face. "Josie." He said in a soft low voice. She refused to meet his hand with her own and instead balled it up into a fist. "Josie. Take my hand." Her hand began to shake a bit. "Come on." One by one her fingers popped out and her arm lifted to meet his. "Josie." Their hands touched.

"What Wayne?"

"I'm totally and completely...messing with you." Wayne's smile exploded from ear to ear and he pressed the photo hard against his chest with his right palm flat out across it.

The next moment both Josie and Wayne stood face to face with Mr. Fairweather in all his perfection.

"Make sure to get my good side now." Mr. Fairweather spoke to the person with the camera.

"Every side is your good side." Mrs. Fairweather walked out from a dressing room in an elegant and tight evening gown. "Especially this one." As she passed behind Mr. Fairweather, she smacked him on his butt.

"Oh!" Mr. Fairweather cried out in painful glee.

"Gross, Mom!" A high-pitched voice shot out from behind Josie and Wayne. They whipped around to see who it was and found themselves staring about a foot over the head of a young boy with the camera in his hand.

"Now, son. One day you'll understand what love is and you'll be doing the same thing." Mrs. Fairweather addressed the boy. "Just not to your father."

The boy fumbled with the camera. It was about two sizes too big for his hands.

"I'm serious about my good side. The last few photos you took of me there seemed to be something...flat going on with my chin." Mr. Fairweather tapped underneath his chin. The boy hung his head. Wayne and Josie weren't sure which way to focus their attention and ended up just glancing back and forth as if they were watching a tennis match. "I absolutely dread low angles."

Mrs. Fairweather let out a forced cough in Mr. Fairweather's direction then nodded her head toward the boy. Mr. Fairweather stopped his exploration of vanity and noticed the upset child.

"Right." He knelt to the boy's level. "Come here, Son." The boy walked over slowly, passing between Wayne and Josie. "I didn't mean to hurt your feelings. Perhaps I should have put it better. Think about it this way, your photos can always be better. You just must keep working at it. There's nothing to be upset about if you don't get it right the first time or the first thousand times. What's important is that you don't give up. So, I'll give you a little tip. Try changing your perspective. You might be surprised what you see." Mr. Fairweather rubbed the boy's head and gently pushed him back over where he had stood to take the photo in the first place.

Wayne watched the boy walk by. For a moment time seemed to stand still. "No."

"What?" Josie looked up at him.

"Can't be."

"What?" Josie stared daggers at Wayne.

"Maybe?"

"Wayne."

"Then who?"

"Okay, you're going to fill me in or I'm leaving this memory."

"I think that boy..." Wayne watched as the boy looked around the room with the camera to his eye pointing it in all sorts of directions. "...is the Professor. That boy is Arnold."

The boy stopped with the camera pointed through Wayne and Josie at Mr. and Mrs. Fairweather. He then lifted the camera up above his hand and looked up at the out of reach viewfinder and back at the lovely couple. Then he looked behind himself at a dumbwaiter. He brought the camera down and let it hang from its strap around his neck and walked over to the dumbwaiter and opened it.

"What are you doing, son?" Mrs. Fairweather asked.

The boy hoisted himself up into the compartment and turned around bringing the camera up to his eye. "I'm changing my perspective."

"That's my boy." Mr. Fairweather showed off his charming smile.

"Sir, Ma'am. Are you too just about ready? The President is waiting." Morese stood just a few feet behind them, tux and all.

"Oh! We should get the whole gang in here. What do you say, dear?" Mrs. Fairweather joyously said while rubbing Mr. Fairweather's arm.

"That's a smashing idea. Morese, get everyone in here."

The rest of the staff came in and took their respective positions. The young boy pressed the shutter and the flash cracked loudly right at Wayne and Josie who stood perfectly in front of their gender specific counterparts in the most obvious juxtaposition possible.

Chapter 30

The party downstairs raged on with a good helping of gossip about why their gracious host repeatedly disappeared. The Fairweathers had always been quite the social butterflies and while they may have only spent, but a couple minutes at a time with each guest, they managed to have a personal moment with them all. Wayne and Josie, on the other hand, stood in the middle of the closet room alone. The ghosts of the picture were gone.

"The dumbwaiter."

"He brought you pigs in a blanket instead of little smokies. It's an honest mistake. Doesn't constitute an insult." Josie shook her finger at Wayne.

"No. The dumbwaiter in the house."

"Exactly. Who else would I be talking about? I'm fairly sure you and I haven't been off the property together in the mere twenty-four hours we've known each other."

"Okay. If I say it one more time, will you promise not to make a joke about it?"

"Maybe." Josie dug her foot into the floor in a tiny kneading motion.

"Josie."

"Okay. Fine. I'll stop." She stomped her foot into her softly kneaded spot.

"That is how we get into the study. The dumbwaiter!" Wayne's finger could have shot a hole in the wall with the speed in which he flung his hand.

"I doubt he has the key."

"Josie!"

Josie brought her crossed fingers out from behind her back. "You should really work on your detective skills. There are like ten mirrors in this room and I could easily see myself doing that in most of them."

Wayne looked around to confirm and even in a room with the intention getting dressed, it was a rather obnoxious number of mirrors. They were of all sizes and hung at various levels for specific and quite individual purposes. There were the standard full body mirrors to view oneself entirely and just as they are, nothing like a funhouse mirror, even though that wouldn't be surprising. There was one hung high near the hats, obviously to just check out how your hats fit. A couple were down built into the footboards for checking your shoes. A quite small one near a thin drawer probably to check out your rings, bracelets, or watches. Two different face heights to view how your glasses look on your face. These mirrors all came in his and hers like monogrammed towels. Wayne looked at one of the full body mirrors and couldn't figure out why that one alone couldn't do the same job as all the rest. "Can we move forward now?"

"Yes." She presented both her hands to him. "No jokes."

"Thank you. And toes don't count." Wayne rushed past Josie to the wall where the dumbwaiter was in the photo memory. He looked and slid his hands all over the walls but couldn't find the door. "Dammit! Did they seal that up too?"

"Who's the dumbwaiter now?" Josie quipped. Wayne snapped around fast enough to break a sweat and gave her the evil eye. "I mean, haven't you seen like anything like ever? Look behind the giant sock shelf with the two cute little sock mirrors." Josie gestured as if her hand was a floppy fish to point at everything she was talking about at once. "That wasn't there in the picture memory. Picto Memory. Pic-Memory, Memory Pic, PicMem."

"Hush!" Wayne paused, turned around slowly, and found himself face to face with an exceptionally large shelf filled with a ridiculous number of socks. "Wow. Mr. Fairweather's Christmases must have socked." Wayne waited for a laugh. "Get it?"

"You're better than that." Josie patted Wayne on the shoulder.

"I guess I just push it." Wayne pushed into the right side of the shelf and nothing happened. Nothing at all. The shelf didn't move an inch. "What the hell?"

"It must be on a hinge." Josie walked over and pulled at the left side, but it didn't budge.

"Who is the dumbwaiter now?"

Josie stopped and blew her tousled hair up and out of her eyes. Wayne strolled over and noticed scratch marks on the wall to the right of the shelf.

"Look! It must only be able to move one direction." Wayne went to the left side of the shelf and examined it before getting it wrong again. He pushed on the left side of the shelf and it moved revealing the hidden dumbwaiter.

"We found it." Josie bobbed over and stood next to Wayne and they both stared at the tiny door on the wall.

"I don't think we'll both fit in there." Wayne said.

"Don't worry. It's all you. That thing looks like a death trap."

"How do you figure?"

"Ummm. It's been hidden behind a shelf for who knows how long." Josie walked over and opened the door and slightly poked her head inside and looked up. "Ropes have got to be rotten by now. Yep, definitely rotten. I'm sure of that."

"What is this?" Wayne joined her. "Miss. Josie afraid of adventure?" Wayne's confidence was skyrocketing.

"No," Josie turned to him, "Living is an adventure. Death is the end."

Wayne's confidence ran away. "Oh."

"Now, what are you waiting for? Get in." Josie patted Wayne on the back.

"But what about the ropes?"

"You'll be fine." Josie helped Wayne up and into the tiny box compartment. "It's only one floor. Fall won't be too long." She smiled and shut the door then placed her hand over a button on a brass panel like the rest of the ones around the house, but this one only had two buttons. Up and down. She pressed down.

Chapter 31

It was dark inside the compartment. "Why isn't there a light in here?" Wayne thought out loud as the old and slow gears moved him down into what he hoped would be Mr. Fairweather's study or else he'd feel incredibly stupid for cramming himself into the death trap he was currently riding. Aches and creeks of the old wood ushered in the just realized fear that maybe the dumbwaiter wasn't meant to hold an adult man weighing in at roughly one hundred and seventy pounds. "At least if I fall it won't be very far." Wayne justified. "Unless there's a basement. Or knowing this place, six basements." A loud pop echoed out and the compartment shook. Wayne braced himself and closed his eyes for what he was now sure would be a lengthy fall.

It took a moment for Wayne to realize the dumbwaiter had stopped. He was there. If they were right about this then upon opening the door, he would be staring straight into Mr. Fairweather's chard, destroyed, and for whatever reason forbidden study. "Okay, Wayne. When you open this door it's only going to be a mess of a fire. Nothing special. Anything you have built up in your head just squash it down and have realistic expectations. It's just a room. This is meeting your heroes. It's going to be a disappointment. Prepare yourself." His fingers felt around the door for the handle. After rubbing his hands over the entire surface of what he was pretty sure was the door, the panic of realizing there was no handle on the inside sunk in. He scrambled and pulled his phone out of his pocket and used the glow of the screen to look around. Nothing. He tapped in his passcode and typed a quick text to Josie. No handle inside. I'm stuck. Bring me up! The bubbles of her response danced across his screen for a while then disappeared. "What? No!" The bubbles returned shortly after. "Don't do that!"

Josie responded, "There's no lock or latch. Just press your hands flat against the door and slide it up. Duh! Wayne felt as dumb as missing the H in school during his third-grade spelling bee. He turned his phone again to the door panel and pressed his hand flat against the grain of the wood. It took up a surprising amount of strength to make it slide up and open. With claustrophobia kicking in he wasted no time getting out of the compartment and into the room with haste. Immediately his attention darted to his phone so he could send off another text to Josie. Made it. Thanks! This was accompanied by a Gif of a Labrador retriever wiping its brow with a handkerchief.

His trapped in the dumbwaiter moment had completely distracted him from his main goal and as he stood in the center of the room he failed to notice the distinct lack of fire damage and the abundant presence of finely crafted furniture and carefully curated collectables and treasures that adorned the walls and shelves. It wasn't until the not so distant flushing sound of a toilet did, he look up and was made aware of the rather unmistakable odor of a fine cigar and the dim glow of light leaking out from under a door marked WC.

Was he inside a picture again? The door marked WC opened and the light behind it flicked off. A puff of smoke billowed out and as it faded it revealed the visage of none other than Mr. Fairweather.

"There you are my boy. I was wondering what was taking you so long." Mr. Fairweather took a long drag of his cigar and made his way over to his reading chair made from a dark wood and a rich red leather with brass beads circling the front of the arms.

Wayne turned to see who he was talking to and to his surprise there was no one there.

"I'm talking to you, kid. My Valentino looks good on you. Or should I say, your Valentino."

Wayne slowly turned back to Mr. Fairweather. "You can see me?"

"Usually it's the ghost who asks that question. But, yes. Plain as day." Mr. Fairweather sat down and placed his cigar gently on the edge of an ashtray with the seal of the President of the United States of America on it. A subtle dusting of ash fell dead center. His hand then moved to a fine crystal glass filled with a dark liquor of some sort. "It's scotch. Go ahead and pour yourself a glass. I bet you could probably use one. Your curious silent narration is screaming in my ear."

Wayne made his way to the bar cart and helped himself to a sizable pour of what he assumed was high dollar stuff. Gripping the bottle, his hand shook, and the neck of the bottle rattled against the rim of the glass.

"It's forty dollars a glass. Can we do away with the mysterious lead ins about your surroundings already? I've been waiting some time to have a chat with you, and I'd like to get it done within this century. Or at least what time we have left in it. No tellin' when those dirty Ruskies will drop the big one on us."

"What year do you think it is?" Wayne sat across from Mr. Fairweather.

"Why, it's 1971. Don't be absurd!"

"Um, add about fifty years." Wayne revealed delicately.

A big toothy grin stretched across Mr. Fairweather's face. "Of course. I'm playing with you. Come on. I've been cooped up in this dusty casket of memories for decades. Give a guy a bit of fun will ya?"

"So, you're a ghost?" Wayne stuttered.

"Yes and no. A ghost wouldn't be able to enjoy a fine Cuban or request a nice 1987 vintage to mix things up when he's had a bit too much scotch. However, a living person would likely be able to walk over to that ornate door and open it right up and join his fellow compatriots for a night of joyous festivities. I suppose you could say I'm a prisoner of time."

"But I watched you burn alive."

"Ahh. You found the special albums. Curious technology isn't it? Shame it couldn't be reproduced. Nicola would have made millions. But back to the point at hand. Yes, you did witness my fiery demise. However, this wouldn't be an effective study if I had not done any actual studying in it. Those books over on that shelf contain centuries of knowledge from the greatest minds the world has ever known and quite a few it never had the pleasure to. At least on the public stage. In those pages I had discovered a way to preserve my consciousness for all time, much like those magic photos, but this way I could interact with those who I came in contact with. Unfortunately, I made a terrible miscalculation."

"What did you do?"

"You see I poured myself a glass of tequila after a long evening of scotch drinking. Lost my faculties and instead of putting my cigar on the ashtray FDR had gifted me, I laid it down on my research causing a great fire."

"You got too drunk and burned yourself alive?"

"Well, you make it sound terrible when you put it that way. There's a bit more to it. You see I had already built a prototype of my memory chamber right here in this very room. I had planned on making it much larger and perhaps even one day built it into a satellite allowing me to move free throughout the Universe, but with my physical death quickly approaching I had to make a choice and I downloaded myself into the only space I had available, this study."

"But you ultimately drank too much and burned yourself alive."

"Yes, yes, yes. I have a close relationship with alcohol and I sometimes lose track. The important thing to take from this is that it worked!" Mr. Fairweather sat back and took in the moment of pleasure he was having telling someone new about his accomplishment.

"Mrs. Fairweather was devastated. She lived the rest of her years traveling the world alone." Wayne was visually upset. The wrinkles and creases already forming on his young face were growing fond of each other and smashed up nice and close.

"You do see how that doesn't sound all that terrible."

"She loved you."

"My boy. You must understand that I loved her very much. I still do. However, her and I made an agreement early on that the adventure, whatever it may be, was always more important."

Silence fell over the room. The two men busied themselves with their drinks.

"Why is no one allowed in here?" Wayne broke the silence.

"Well that's a bit complicated. You see, the spell I used only made my physical appearance visible to someone from my bloodline. The same, goes for this room. To anyone else it would just be an empty and charred mess."

"Bloodline? Wait. What?"

Wayne ran the words the crazy old man just spoke through his computer like mind. A computer small enough to fit inside the skull of a human man. The stuff of science fiction. What ever could he mean?

"Then how am I seeing all this?"

"Well, I suppose genius has been known to skip a generation. That or I must have made another miscalculation." Mr. Fairweather grabbed a notebook and began flipping through pages frantically. He was mad with curiosity.

"Wait a minute." Wayne grabbed Mr. Fairweather by the wrist and was surprised at how real he felt. He took a deep breath in. Then he let it all out. "Are you my Grandpa?"

"I prefer Grandfather. Or if you must Paw Paw."

Wayne leaped from his chair like a cat scared of a cucumber followed by a hurried pacing of the room. "That explains so much!" He made his way back around to Mr. Fairweather. "Why would a dying old woman just give me all of this. Because she's your grandma idiot." His eyes met with Mr. Fairweather's. "Sorry. Grandmother. Maw maw."

"Settle down before you blow a fuse. And it's Mamma."

Wayne sat, but remained on the edge of his seat. "Oh, man. I have so many questions. Where do I start? I know, how about this one? Why didn't you take me in when my parents died?"

"Straight shooter. Must be my blood after all."

"Then shoot straight with me. I was a kid! I had to go live with strangers!" Wayne gripped his glass so tight it might have broken any second.

"Wayne. As I implied when you came in here, I've been waiting some time to talk to you." Mr. Fairweather leaned in close to Wayne. "Those people who died in that car wreck weren't your parents. The Morris' were a family your parents knew well and trusted. They sent you to live with them when you were born. The stuff your father was into," Mr. Fairweather paused. "It was too dangerous for a child to be around. Too dangerous to live here even. I'm deeply sorry, my boy."

Wayne's world warped around him like one would see in a movie when the background seems to distort around the hero who remains the same size. A technique known as the dolly zoom performed by the simultaneous action of zooming the lens of a camera in and physically moving the camera away from the subject. That, that is how Wayne felt in the moment.

"I bet that is a lot to take in, but I felt it was especially important for you to hear it from me. It's why I asked Martha to withhold the information from you. That's why she made it so that everyone would withhold it from you. Down to my last will and testament."

"So, you can talk to others?"

"Through letters yes and my brilliant wife discovered a spell to allow true love to see me. That was her, by the way."

"What if I never cared to come in here? I'd never have known."

"That was a calculated risk. You see you're a Fairweather, my boy. You have a naturally inquisitive mind. I knew once you saw the door with all of its carvings, you'd make a series of associations that would ultimately lead you here. And of course, I couldn't make it easy for you. What's the fun in that?" Mr. Fairweather took a big sip from his scotch. "Also, if it took too long then I was going to just have Morsese or Ginger tell you. I told her to nudge you toward the photos after all. Oops. I cheated."

"So, the people who raised me till I was eight, they're not my parents. Does that mean my parents are still alive?"

"That I am not sure of. I lost contact with your father long ago. We would write regularly, but then the letters stopped coming. He never actually made the trip down here like you did. All I have of him is an old box filled with ink put to paper. The last letter was highly censored leading me to believe they are linked up with a military outfit of some kind. He was always chasing something and your mother, well, she was always chasing him."

"Adventure was more important than me?" Wayne stood and walked across the room and pulled back the curtains where the window was only to find it covered from the outside with brick. "Right. Of course. A guy can't even stare longingly out a window when he learns his parents may still be alive and didn't want him."

"Oh, they wanted you. No doubt about that. But you were safer with Mr. and Mrs. Morris. Your parents cared for you so much, they did not want to see you meet the same fate as I or fall into the same obsession as they. Sending you off to lead a boring and average life was what they thought was best."

"Safe? My parents...the Morris's died in a car wreck. Safe."

"The world is naturally unsafe, that is true. But it's far safer than the world your parents and I involved ourselves in."

"Then why bring me in now? Why not just leave me to spend the rest of my days with a guy named Mark who'd rather pay me to hang out with him while he donates blood instead of just doing it alone like most people? Why did Mrs. Fairweather bring me into all this?"

"Because. A Fairweather must always be in control of the estate. Without our bloodline here the oddities that exist here would pose both a great danger to the outside world and a great danger to themselves. If you don't believe me just look at Ginger. She looks a bit younger now than when you first arrived, does she not?"

Wayne placed his glass on the desk to his right. Deep thought furrowed his brow. "Yeah, I thought I was crazy."

"Not crazy. She stays young as the youngest residing here. Don't worry, she only goes back to twenty-three. Without one of us she would parish."

"Heavy."

"Indeed."

"Man, I don't know. This is all starting to sound like a lot of responsibility." Wayne could no longer sit still and broke out into a nervous pace with no clear direction.

"That's unfortunate because I'm not quite done."

"What now? Are you going to tell me that if I don't marry Josie then the cell tower will send out a beacon across the galaxy that will call a violent alien race to Earth and destroy everything?"

"Not quite that. However, you two would make a great match. Martha simply adored her. No, I want you to find your parents. Living or dead. Living preferably. For their sake. And if they do happen to be deceased then bring their bodies home to be buried with the rest of the family."

"Where would I even start?"

"Well, this box of letters detailing your father's adventures that I mentioned not five minutes ago might be a good place. He has likely left clues in them. Always so intelligent that one. I wouldn't be surprised if he's hiding out at some University somewhere molding young minds."

"Teaching?"

"It's a noble profession really. A bit too stale for my taste, but perhaps he finally found peace in his journeys and settled down."

"I have to go." Wayne walked over to the dumbwaiter.

"Oh, so soon?" Mr. Fairweather slightly shifted in his chair to lean somewhat in Wayne's direction. "I didn't mean right now. But I understand. The party rages on."

"I'm sorry. Will you be here if I come back?"

"Oh, I suppose so. I've already done my grocery shopping for the week and have some reading to catch up on. Maybe finish that jigsaw puzzle I started forty years ago."

"Seriously?"

"No, my boy. Go. Adventure is around every corner and you mustn't keep it waiting."

"Thank you." Wayne was halfway into the compartment.

"Speak nothing of it. Simply doing my grandfatherly duty."

Wayne smiled and said nothing then crammed himself into the dumbwaiter and pulled his phone out and sent a text to Josie. Bring me up. I have big news.

Chapter 32

"He's what? They're what?" Josie's feet struggled to keep up with Wayne's as he barreled down out of the closet room and down the hall.

"Yeah." Wayne's face couldn't decide whether it wanted to be determined or excited as he made his way back to the party, adjusting his outfit as he went.

"You're like a combination of Spider-Man and Superman."

"Yeah, wait what?" Wayne stopped dead in his tracks and turned around to face Josie. Josie nearly ran right into him, stopping only inches from his face.

"Spider-Man's parents left him with his aunt and uncle and disappeared for some adventure or science related thing and Superman has a big ice fort where the collected memories and knowledge of his father are stored for him to seek advice from whenever he needs it."

"'Your life is unoriginal and there's no point in going on' is all you had to say." With the wind from his sails depleting slowly, Wayne's mind entered a questioning state.

Josie placed both her hands-on Wayne's pouty face. "Aww, I'm sorry. I didn't mean to pour too much syrup on your pancakes. Perk up. This is exciting! You're like a superhero."

"Yeah, you're right. I'm better than those guys anyway."

"Well…"

"Josie."

"You're right. Hell yeah you are!" She quickly posed her fists on her hips in a very Superman stance. ADHD surged in her mind and her expression changed to genuine care. "Aww. Was it so good meeting and talking and hugging your Grandpa?"

Wayne stopped. "Hug? I didn't even shake his hand. I just grabbed him by the wrist like a jerk. Whatever, it can wait." Wayne continued.

"You didn't even touch his face to feel all his years?" Josie hurried after.

"The crazy thing is I don't think I'm going to have to look very hard for my dad." The adrenaline was slicing Wayne's emotions every which way.

"Oh yeah?" Josie said out of breath.

"Yeah, like this whole thing has been about me seeking adventure, but maybe my boring lazy life was the way to go about it the whole time."

"You don't honestly think your dad is just going to come to you. Do you? Please say you don't."

"I think he already has. Come with me." Wayne offered her his hand. "I'm ready to party now."

"Oh dear." Josie squeaked out as Wayne pulled her down the hall and toward the staircase.

Chapter 33

Wayne and Josie stood hand in hand back to the top of the stairs and surveyed the crowd of people.

"Third time's a charm." Josie made a joke. "Are you sure you're ready to greet your people?"

"I have one thing I need to do first." Wayne didn't have to look far before he found Arnold standing by the bar and he rushed down the stairs to him. "Arnold." Wayne said very respectfully.

"Wayne." Arnold mocked.

Wayne's heartbeat to the rhythm guitar of Eye of the Tiger while his feet tapped out the lead. Arnold starred at Wayne with his whiskey glass perched on his lips as Wayne internally got through the intro and into the first verse. Choking on his nerves Wayne finally coughed out a frenzied and rushed, "Areyoumydad?"

Arnold swallowed his current sip and set the glass on the bar. O'Connor went to pour another as his instincts were sparked to do, however, Arnold calmly motioned for him to stop. "Wayne, what I am about to say may come as a great shock to you and I want you to be prepared for that because the answer to your question is a resounding and unequivocal, no. I am not your father." Without shifting his gaze from Wayne's eyes, he tapped the bar twice and only then did O'Connor pour another. Two fingers worth. This unusual behavior combined with the unfulfilling news he just dropped had Wayne off kilter.

"But Mr. Fairweather is your dad and he's my Grandfather."

"Mr. Fairweather is not my dad." Arnold scanned the room as if searching for prey. "My Dad was a car salesman in Akron, Ohio. What would give you a hairbrained idea like that?"

"You're the boy from the photo."

"What photo?"

"Well you're the one taking the photo I guess." Wayne scrambled his palms through the lining of his pockets searching for the photo.

"What photo?"

"The one you told us to change our perspective with." His frantic hands were coming up empty.

"I'm drunk. I was just bullshitting with you."

"But Mr. Fairweather said the same thing to you...or the boy." Wayne gave up his search for the photo. He looked to Josie who responded from nearby with a clueless look and a mouth half full of fried pickles.

"It's a common thing to say to someone when they can't find what they're looking for in the way they're currently looking for it." Arnold spotted Ginger from across the room. "I'm an educator. Guiding young minds is sort of my thing."

"So, you're not my real father?" Frustration began to set in on Wayne's face.

"No." Arnold's primary attention was now on Ginger.

"And you're not related to the Fairweathers."

"No." His responses to Wayne were now peppered with a hint of misdirected flirtation.

"And I still have to go searching for my actual parents."

"I don't know what you're talking about, but I guess so." Arnold's body shifted where he stood, screaming to get out of the current dead-end conversation Wayne had brought to him.

"I really jumped to conclusions on that one. The saying, Mr. F saying you might be a professor now, your excessive drinking..."

"Whoa!" Arnold finished off his glass and brought his full attention back to Wayne. "It's just a special occasion...most days." O'Connor filled his glass without Arnold even handing it to him. "I did sleep with your mother once."

"What?"

"Long before she met your dad. It's how I know them." With the weight of his confession off his chest he began to creep back on the flirtation trail. "Also, you think I'm such a shitty father that I would meet you all those years ago in Texas and let you tell me all about how your parents died and how fucked up you are now and not tell you I was in fact your father? Then come here and do it again under a name you don't know? Jesus, kid. Thanks! Now if you'll excuse me."

"My mentor is a drunken creep." Wayne tapped the bar and O'Connor served him one of the same as Arnold.

"You met me in a biker bar in Texas. What did you think? Also, I'm not your mentor either." Arnold glanced at Wayne's glass. "Don't drink what I drink. Anymore."

"It's whiskey. Tons of people drink it. It's not some special Arnold only drink." Wayne took a sip. "Or should I say, Tennessee Smith? And you're totally my mentor. If you're not my father. You're my mentor.

"No. I'm not."

"You are."

"No."

"Yes."

"No."

"Yes."

The two men stared at each other waiting for the other to say the next word.

A loud booming voice shook the house from outside. "BOY!"

"What was that?" Arnold reached his glass back to O'Connor to top it off.

"Oh, god." Wayne looked back at Josie. The look on her face told him all he needed to know about who it was.

Wayne, Arnold, and Josie ran outside followed by the rest of the party guests.

Once they reached the steps of the entry, they saw a smoldering, angry, and still wet former Fire Bear standing on the lawn.

"Friend of yours?" Arnold asked as he reached over and stole a drink from a nearby party guest's hand. He started alternating sips from each of his glasses in a nervous manner.

"That's Fire Bear." Josie chimed in. "Wayne kicked his butt."

"You fought that?" Arnold pointed with both his glasses.

"Yep." Wayne tapped his foot nervously.

"Doesn't seem so fiery."

"Yeah. I sort of snuffed him out." Wayne could feel all of the eyes from the party in a tennis match between himself and the extremely perturbed, ash dusted beast.

"You took everything from me! You destroyed my home. Now I will destroy yours." Fire Bear bellowed.

"He doesn't seem happy, Wayne. What are you going to do about it?" Arnold downed the fruity cocktail he'd stolen and almost choked on a cherry garnish.

"Not sure yet." Wayne looked around at all the party guests who were looking to their host for leadership. Fire Bear may not be on fire anymore, but he was still a bear.

"Still got that tattoo?" Arnold fixed his gaze on Fire Bear.

"Aren't they permanent?" Wayne responded also fixed on Fire Bear.

Arnold began rolling up his right sleeve, revealing all his tattoos.

"What's going on?" Wayne noticed Arnolds action.

"Get ready." Arnold cracked his neck and finished rolling his sleeve.

"I will burn this manor to the ground!" With arms stretched wide Fire Bear's arms engulfed in flame. Everyone gasped or screamed and some of the guests even passed out. Josie held her arms across her chest and got close to Wayne. Arnold slowly stepped behind her. O'Connor, Ginger, Santiago, and Morese also grouped together, waited for Wayne to do, or say something.

"Manor?" Wayne half turned and looked at the building behind him. "This is a manor?" Everyone looked at Wayne with grave concern and confusion. "I've been calling it a house this whole time."

Tyler Huffman

Wayne's Manner

About the Author

In addition to being an author, Tyler pens screenplays, is an actor, and an accomplished photographer with his work  installed in the Tulsa International Airport and featured internationally in galleries including Laurent Gallery in Malborne, Australia. His first feature screenplay for "A Great North Christmas" was produced in 2021 by Princ Films and shot in Prince George, Canada.

tyler@thetylerhuffman.com
www.thetylerhuffman.com

Wayne's Manner

Made in the USA
Coppell, TX
25 January 2024